KNOWLEDGMENTS

always, I am indebted to the people who helped make this book happen: itors Patricia Lee Gauch and Tamra Tuller; agents Kendra Marcus nd Minju Chang; my many writer friends, including Moira Donohue, Maureen Lewis, Susan Barry Fulop, Kathy May, Anne Marie Pace, Fran Slayton, and Julie Swanson; and, of course, my always supportive and wonderful husband, Bill, and awesome children, Gavin and Fiona, who all deserve special tribute, as does my sister, Jan, my biggest cheerleader. Thanks to all of you.

PATRICIA LEE GAUCH, EDITOR

PHILOMEL BOOKS A division of Penguin Young Readers Group. Published by The Penguin Group. Penguin Group (USA) Inc., 375 Hudson Street, New York, NY 10014, U.S.A. Penguin Group (Canada), 90 Eglinton Avenue East, Suite 700, Toronto, Ontario M4P 2Y3, Canada (a division of Pearson Penguin Canada Inc.). Penguin Books Ltd, 80 Strand, London WC2R 0RL, England. Penguin Ireland, 25 St. Stephen's Green, Dublin 2, Ireland (a division of Penguin Books Ltd). Penguin Group (Australia), 250 Camberwell Road, Camberwell, Victoria 3124, Australia (a division of Pearson Australia Group Pty Ltd). Penguin Books India Pvt Ltd, 11 Community Centre, Panchsheel Park, New Delhi—110 017, India. Penguin Group (NZ), 67 Apollo Drive, Rosedale, North Shore 0632, New Zealand (a division of Pearson New Zealand Ltd). Penguin Books (South Africa) (Pty) Ltd, 24 Sturdee Avenue, Rosebank, Johannesburg 2196, South Africa. Penguin Books Ltd, Registered Offices: 80 Strand, London WC2R 0RL, England.

Published simultaneously in Canada. Printed in the United States of America. Design by Semadar Megged. Text set in 12.5-point Elegant Garamond.

Library of Congress Cataloging-in-Publication Data
Erskine, Kathryn. Mockingbird / Kathryn Erskine. p. cm. Summary: Ten-year-old Caitlin, who has Asperger's syndrome, struggles to understand emotions, show empathy, and make friends at school, while at home she seeks closure by working on a project with her father. [1. Asperger's syndrome—Fiction. 2. Empathy—Fiction. 3. Schools—Fiction. 4. Death—Fiction. 5. School shootings—Fiction. 6. Family life—Virginia—Fiction. 7. Virginia—Fiction.] I. Title. PZ7.E7388Moc 2010 [Fic]—dc22 2009006741

ISBN 978-0-399-25264-8
10 9 8 7 6 5 4 3

MOCKINGBIR

MOK'ING-BÛRD

KATHRYN ERSKINE

PHILOMEL BOOKS
AN IMPRINT OF PENGUIN GROUP (USA) INC.

*In hopes that we may all
    understand each other better*

CHAPTER **1**

DEVON'S CHEST

IT LOOKS LIKE A ONE-WINGED bird crouching in the corner of our living room. Hurt. Trying to fly every time the heat pump turns on with a click and a groan and blows cold air onto the sheet and lifts it up and it flutters for just a moment and then falls down again. Still. Dead.

Dad covered it with the gray sheet so I can't see it, but I know it's there. And I can still draw it. I take my charcoal pencil and copy what I see. A grayish square-ish thing that's almost as tall as me. With only one wing.

Underneath the sheet is Devon's Eagle Scout project. It's the chest Dad and Devon are making so he'll be ready to teach other Boy Scouts how to build a chest. I feel all around the sheet just to be sure his chest is underneath. It's cold and hard and stiff on the outside and cavernous on the inside. My Dictionary says CAVernous means filled with cavities or hollow areas. That's what's on the inside of Devon's chest. Hollow areas. On the outside is the part that looks like the bird's broken wing because the sheet hangs off of it loosely. Under the sheet is a piece of wood that's going to be the door once Dad and Devon finish the chest. Except now I don't know how they can. Now that Devon is gone. The bird will be trying to fly but never getting anywhere. Just floating and falling. Floating and falling.

The gray of outside is inside. Inside the living room. Inside the chest. Inside me. It's so gray that turning on a lamp is too sharp and it hurts. So the lamps are off. But it's still too bright. It should be black inside and that's what I want so I put my head under the sofa cushion where the green plaid fabric smells like Dad's sweat and Devon's socks

2

and my popcorn and the cushion feels soft and heavy on my head and I push deeper so my shoulders and chest can get under it too and there's a weight on me that holds me down and keeps me from floating and falling and floating and falling like the bird.

CHAPTER 2

LOOK AT THE PERSON

CAITLIN, DAD SAYS. THE WHOLE
town is upset by what happened. They want to
help.

How?

They want to be with you. Talk to you. Take
you places.

I don't want to be with them or talk to them
or go places with them.

He sighs. *They want to help you deal with life, Caitlin . . . without Devon.*

I don't know what this means but the people come to our house. I wish I could hide in Devon's room but I'm not allowed in there now. Not since The Day Our Life Fell Apart and Dad slammed Devon's door shut and put his head against it and cried and said, *No no no no no.* So I can't go to my hidey-hole in Devon's room anymore and I miss it.

I try to hide in my room and draw but Dad comes and gets me.

There are so many voices in our house. Voices from Devon's Boy Scout troop. I recognize their green pants. And the nice things they say about Devon.

Voices of relatives. Dad introduces me to them. He says, *You remember . . .* and then he says a name.

I say, *No,* because I don't remember.

Dad says to Look At The Person so I look quickly at a nose or a mouth or an ear but I still don't remember.

One voice says, *I'm your second cousin.*

Another says, *Wasn't it a beautiful memorial service?*

Another says, *I love your drawings. You're a very talented artist. Will you draw something for me?*

One even says, *Aren't you lucky to have so many relatives?*
I don't feel lucky but they keep coming.

Relatives we hardly saw when Devon was here so how can they help?

Neighbors like the man who yelled at Devon to get off his lawn. How can he help?

People from school. Mrs. Brook my counselor. Miss Harper the principal. All my teachers since kindergarten except my real fifth-grade teacher because she left after what happened at Devon's school. I don't Get It because nothing bad happened at James Madison Elementary School so why did she have to leave? Now Mrs. Johnson is my teacher. She didn't even know Devon except she watched him play basketball, she says. Twice. I've watched the LA Lakers play more than twice. I don't try to help them.

Caitlin. If you ever want to talk about what happened you just let me know, Mrs. Johnson says.

That's what Mrs. Brook is for, I tell her.

Maybe we could all sit down together.

Why?

So we know where you're coming from.

I look around the living room and stare at the sheet-covered chest. *I come from here.*

I'm sorry. I meant so we all know how you're feeling.

Oh. Mrs. Brook knows how I'm feeling so you can find out from her. I would be superfluous. My Dictionary says suPER-fluous means exceeding what is sufficient or necessary.

I just thought it would be nice to take some time to sit and chat.

I shake my head. *SuPERfluous also means marked by wastefulness.*

Well . . . okay then, she says. *I suppose I can talk with Mrs. Brook.*

Mrs. Brook says you can talk with her anytime because her door is always open, I tell Mrs. Johnson. *Actually it's almost always closed. But if you knock then she remembers to open it.*

Thank you Caitlin.

She doesn't move. This means she is waiting for me to say something. I hate that. It makes my underarms prickle and get wet. I almost start sucking my sleeve like I do at recess but then I remember. *You're welcome,* I say.

She moves away.

I got it right! I go to the refrigerator and put a smiley face sticker on my chart under YOUR MANNERS. Seven more and I get to watch a video.

When I turn away from the fridge I see a puffy blue marshmallow wall in front of me. It smells of apple cinnamon Pop-Tarts and breathes noisily. It's another neighbor or relative. I don't know which. Her hands are shaking. One hand has a tissue and the other hand she holds out to me. There is a white circle in it. *Would you like this candy?*

I don't know. I have never had her candy before so I don't know if I'll like it. But I like just about every candy in the galaxy. I don't like being trapped by the puffy blue wall like this though.

Take it, she says, and pushes it into my hand.

So I take it just to get her hand off of mine because her hand is squishy and flabby and makes me feel sick.

Have another, she says.

I take it quickly so I won't have to feel her hand again.

She tries to pat my head with the candy hand but I duck.

I run and hide behind Dad. And eat the candy. They are

mints. I wish they were gummy worms because that's my favorite but I Deal With It. The good thing is I can't talk when my mouth is full because that's rude so if I keep my mouth full I can be in my own Caitlin world.

When I finish the candy I still don't want to talk so I push my head under Dad's sweater and feel the warmth of his chest as he breathes up and down and I smell his Gillette Cool Wave Antiperspirant and Deodorant. He doesn't even say, *No Caitlin,* and pull me out. He lets me stay there and pats my head through the sweater. If it's through the sweater I don't mind. Otherwise I don't like anyone to touch me. Dad talks to the world outside the sweater and his voice makes a low hummy-vibratey feel. I close my eyes and wish I could stay here forever.

CHAPTER **3**

LET'S TALK ABOUT IT

DAD SAYS IT'S TIME TO GO BACK to school so here I am.

Back in Mrs. Brook's room.

Sitting at the little round table.

I look at the walls and not much has changed except that the mad face on the Facial Expressions Chart now has a mustache. I know because I have looked at that chart about a million times to try to figure out which emotion goes with each face. I'm not very good at it. I have to use the chart because when I look at real faces I don't Get It. Mrs. Brook says people have a hard time understanding me because I have Asperger's so I have to try extra hard to understand them and that means working on emotions.

I'd rather work on drawing.

Hi Caitlin, Mrs. Brook says softly. She still smells like Dial Body Wash.

I look at the chart and nod. This means I'm listening even if there's no eye contact.

So how are you?

I suck on my sleeve and stare at the chart.

How are you feeling?

I stare at the chart some more and hear myself sigh. My stomach feels all yucky like it's at recess which is my worst subject but I take a deep breath and try to Deal With It. Finally I say, *I feel like TiVo.*

She leans across the table toward me. Not too close to my Personal Space because I'll use my words to tell her to back off if she gets too close. *Say again?*

TEE-VO.

What do you mean?

I fast-forward through the bad parts and all of a sudden I'm watching something and I'm not sure how I got there.

She scratches the part in her hair with her forefinger. The rest of her fingers stick up in the air and move like they're waving. Then she stops. *I see,* she says.

I look around the room. *What do you see?* I ask.

I think you'd like to forget about the painful events you've been through.

I want to tell her that I prefer TiVo on mute and I wish she'd cooperate. But if I do it'll start a whole Let's Talk About It discussion so I say nothing.

The funeral must have been very difficult, she says.

I wonder what she means. We sat in church. It was not very difficult. It was like TiVo on mute. Everyone spoke so quietly I could barely hear them and almost no one talked to me. They looked at me which I did not like and some of them even touched me which I hate but no one tried to Start a Conversation with me and no one laughed like crashing glass and there was no lightning movement and no one appeared out of nowhere and nothing happened suddenly.

Let's Talk About It, she says.

I turn around in my chair so I can't see her anymore.

I know it's difficult but you can't keep it all inside. She stops talking but not for long. *Did you cry at the funeral?*

I shake my head. At the funeral a lot of grown-ups cried but I don't know why. Most of them had never even met Devon. I think about how much Dad has been crying and the words jump out of my mouth. *Dad cried.*

Did that upset you?

I grip the back of my chair. *I didn't like it.*

Why not?

I don't know.

Were you sad for him?

I don't know.

Were you afraid?

I don't know.

Did it make you uncomfortable?

I try to think of a different answer than I don't know because Devon says people don't like I don't know all that much. I don't know why. So I try hard to focus on her question. *Did it make you uncomfortable?* I think about what is comfortable. Being completely covered by my purple fleece blanket under my bed or putting my head under the sofa cushion or reading my Dictionary. I did not have any of those things at the funeral. *Yes. I was uncomfortable.*

Why?

I don't know. Please stop asking me questions.

Caitlin. Your father is sad.

I turn back toward the Facial Expressions Chart. I wonder how Mrs. Brook knows what he's feeling right now. And I wonder if I've done something wrong. *Why?*

Her head pokes forward like a turtle before she pulls it back in and says in her Nice Voice, *He misses Devon.*

Oh. MISS is a strange word, I tell her. *Have you ever looked it up in the Dictionary? There is MISS like MISS Harper the principal. There is MISS like you will MISS your bus if you don't hurry because you have to step on every crack. And there is MISS like dead.*

Do you miss Devon?

I don't know.

She does the turtle head jerk again—just barely but I see it.

He's not completely gone anyway, I tell her. I think about his bedroom even though the door is shut and his bike leaning

14

against the back of the house and his chest in the corner of the living room.

Her face squishes up like she's trying to Get It. *That's true,* she says slowly. *A part of Devon will always be with you.*

Which part, I wonder. No parts of his body are left because he was cremated. That means burned up into ashes.

Can you feel him?

I look around the air. I look down at my hands. Are parts of Devon scraping me? Is that what I'm supposed to feel? The heat is blowing from the vent in the ceiling and I feel that. But that's only air from the furnace. Or does it have Devon in it? Where do you go when you get burned up and turn into smoke in the air? Maybe you get sucked into furnace systems and blown out through the vents. I shrug.

Can't you still feel Devon? Mrs. Brook asks again.

Maybe. I'm not sure it's really him though. It could be anyone. What would he feel like?

I mean the things he did for you. The things you did together. You'll miss him but he'll always be with you. Just in a different way.

I don't want him around in a different way. I want him around in the same way. The way he was before. When he makes me popcorn and hot chocolate. And he tells me what to say and what clothes to wear and how not to be weird so kids won't laugh at me. And he plays basketball with me. He always gives me a chance to win by tripping or moving slowly or going the wrong way when I do a fake. I can tell when he's doing something on purpose by looking at his mouth. His lips move a certain way when he's thinking. When he's being sneaky his lips move a different way. But when he's being sneaky he's doing it to be nice to me.

That's the Devon I want. Not the one who is floating around in the air.

A loud country music song starts playing.

It's Mrs. Brook's cell phone.

She doesn't answer.

She's using her Look At The Person behavior to look at me and I don't like it. Also she's not answering the phone. I can't stand the cowboy song noise.

If you don't answer the phone you will MISS your call, I tell her.

She answers but her eyes still Look At The Person while she talks on the phone.

I get under the table to get away from her eyes. Mrs.

Brook always wants me to look in her eyes. She says we can see emotion in people's eyes. I can't. Eyes always look the same to me. People's lips move all the time though. That's where the words come out. I can tell what people say by looking at their lips even though Mrs. Brook says that's not the only way to find out because you can't get a complete picture of what someone means just by looking at their lips. I can. I can read lips.

I look up at the wood on the bottom side of the table.

It's not finished wood.

It's raw wood.

Like Devon's chest.

I touch it. It's rough. I rub my finger across the wood back and forth harder and harder until a splinter cuts me. I hit the splinter back.

There is a drop of blood on the wood now. It is red and it spreads . . . seeping into a crack and bleeding across the unfinished wood.

Like Devon's chest.

No! I rub the wood harder and harder to try to erase the blood but it won't go away.

Caitlin!

I press my finger against the raw wood and rub faster and faster and it hurts but I don't care because I want to stop the blood but it's still there and I can't make it stop!

Caitlin!

I can't stop it!

Caitlin! It's Mrs. Brook calling from somewhere and I feel pulling on my arm but I yank my hand free. *No!* I have to erase the blood! I have to. I have to! I HAVE TO!

I can't see or feel or hear anything except for some screaming far away.

CHAPTER 4

LIFE

I HEARD YOU HAD A TRM AT school today, Dad says.

I stare at the covered chest in the corner. *TRM,* I say, *hmm. That Reminds Me.* I know he doesn't mean that kind of TRM. He means the Tantrum Rage Meltdown kind. But I don't want to talk about it.

He sighs. *Caitlin honey—*

My finger hurt, I say. *That's why.*

I think it was more than your finger.

Also I bumped my head on the table during the TR—when my finger hurt. So it was my finger and my head. Both. That's two things. I continue counting in my head. Three, four, five, six.

I hear Dad's voice but I focus on counting. Seven, eight, nine, ten, eleven. And thinking about stuffed animals. And I want Red Dog so I get up and walk down the hall to my room which is thirteen and a half steps—more if you take little tiptoe steps so you don't step on any of the seams in the wood. I look across at Devon's room and wish wish wish I could go in but I know I can't.

I hear Dad saying my name but he is in another world right now.

Twenty-one, twenty-two, twenty-three, twenty-four.

I push my door open and wade through the clothes and books and papers and pencils and yarn and stickers on my floor and go to my bed where there are one hundred and fifty-three stuffed animals including key chains and Mc-Donald's Happy Meal toys but the one I want is Red Dog and he is sleeping under the bed with my purple fleece blanket because Dad is too loud—thirty-seven, thirty-eight, thirty-nine—and I get under the blanket with Red Dog and we go to sleep while I am still counting.

When I wake up I'm hungry. I look at my Elmo clock. Elmo says it's almost six thirty. I step out into the hall and look at the door across from mine. It's Devon's. Dad keeps it closed since The Day Our Life Fell Apart. I can't open it because Dad always says when the bathroom door is closed you don't open it and when a desk drawer is closed you don't open it and when an envelope is closed you don't open it unless it has your name on it. So I don't open Devon's door.

I wish I could go in though. I wish I could go in and say, *Devon I'm hungry,* and he'd grin so his dimples show and he'd say, *You and me both,* and we'd go find Dad and order pizza because it's Thursday and we'd eat warm drippy extra-cheese pizza in front of *Wheel of Fortune* and *Jeopardy.* That reminds me how hungry I am so I go find Dad.

He's sitting on the sofa staring at my charcoal pencil stain on the carpet.

It's six thirty, I say.

Dad doesn't say anything.

It's six thirty. Time to eat, I tell him, in case he has forgotten what six thirty means.

He still doesn't say anything.

It's six thirty.

He stares at the stain but at least he says something. *I'm not hungry.*

It doesn't matter, I tell him. *It's six thirty.*

He sighs. *Okay. I'm glad you're feeling better now. I'll get dinner ready.*

Just call the pizza guy.

He shakes his head.

It's Thursday.

Let's eat what we have here.

But it's pizza night.

No Caitlin.

I cross my arms. *I don't want that yucky spaghetti casserole again.*

Okay. He gets up slowly like he is a very old toy running out of batteries. *I'll see what we have.*

We have Pop-Tarts.

That's not exactly a healthy dinner.

We have a bag of salad you can eat.

His lips turn down at the ends. *I don't like salad. And we don't have any dressing.*

Yes we do. Applesauce.

So we eat Pop-Tarts and salad with applesauce. Only I pick the salad stuff out of my applesauce and make a pile of green leaves on my napkin. And I keep my applesauce and Pop-Tart totally separate because I don't like food mixing together or colors running into each other. It's too hard to see what you have to Deal With if things start blurring together and getting mushy and turning into each other.

We sit at the kitchen table where I can't see the TV which isn't on anyway. It's too quiet without Devon. Right now I wouldn't even mind watching Fox Five News with the lady who talks so fast and so loud you can't hear what she's saying. All you can do is watch her really big hair moving around and wonder how many spiders make their nests in that thing.

Dad sniffs and I don't want to hear him crying again so I have to be like the Fox Five News lady and fill up the silence. *I wish we could have pizza with Devon,* I say. *It's even Thursday. Pizza day.*

Dad stops eating. *Me too.* He puts his hands together and his fingers grip the backs of his hands hard. He looks at the picture on the wall between the kitchen and living room and stares at it for a while. It's Devon in his Scout uniform at a moving-up ceremony.

Is that his Life picture?

Dad tilts his head at me. This means he doesn't Get It.

Life. In Boy Scouts. Remember? Devon?

Oh. He looks back at the photo of Devon. *Yes. That's when he made his Life rank in Scouts.*

And Eagle comes after Life.

Dad nods and sighs. *He wanted very much to make Eagle.*

From my seat at the kitchen table I can see the corner of the living room where the chest sits. *That's his Eagle project.*

Yes, says Dad. *It was.*

He can't make Eagle if the chest isn't finished.

Dad swallows hard even though he's not eating anything. He gets up from the table and leaves the other half of his Pop-Tart and his salad stuff too.

I don't feel hungry anymore so I put my plate in the

dishwasher. I have to scrape Dad's plate before I put it in the dishwasher. Then I sit down and draw like I do all the time. Devon says if I went a whole day without drawing I would probably die. But that will never happen because I can't go a whole entire day without drawing.

Dad sits back down on the sofa and stares at the pencil stain on the carpet.

CHAPTER **5**

PERSONAL SPACE

I HATE RECESS EVEN THOUGH
Devon says it's supposed to be my favorite subject and there is no recess once you get to middle school so enjoy it now. But I can't enjoy it
because I'm surrounded by sharp screaming
and it's too bright and people's elbows are all
pointy and dangerous and it's hard to breathe
and my stomach always feels really really sick.
I stand and put my arms around me like a force
field and squeeze my eyes almost closed to try

to shut everything out. It doesn't work. I still feel like a Fake Item Box that Mario is going to run over any minute now. I start sucking my shirt cuff that's sticking out of my jacket sleeve.

I see Josh pushing people off of the monkey bars again. He used to be in my class before he got put in the other fifth-grade room because Mrs. Brook says it's better that way. I think so too. Josh used to be just loud but now he's loud and evil. Dad says it's because Josh's cousin was one of the school shooters at Devon's school. The one the police caught right away. And killed. But not before he shot Devon.

Now my heart is pounding loud and I want to moan but Devon says you can't moan or scream or shake your hands up and down or rock or get under a table or spin around over and over in public. Actually you can't do most things over and over in public because that's not normal unless it's something like clapping or laughing but you have to do it only at the right times and places and Devon always tells me. Now I don't know anymore.

My eyes feel hot and itchy and everything is blurry so I remember an okay thing I can do which is to blur colors and shapes so they change into fuzzy and warm instead of sharp and cold. I call it stuffed-animaling. If you take the monkey bars and the people and blur them together they get soft and fluffy and kind just like a stuffed animal. And you can forget about where you are and pretend you're somewhere else like under your bed with your stuffed animals.

I'm stuffed-animaling the playground so well that after a while there's only monkey bars left and one shape that's coming toward me so I stop blurring and suck my sleeve more. Blurring is good for the things you don't want to see but it doesn't work so well for the stuff you actually have to Deal With.

Josh is walking toward me and he's smiling even though he runs into William H.'s Personal Space and knocks him down. You shouldn't walk into someone else's Personal Space. Especially not William H.'s. William H. is autistic. He's in the other fifth-grade class. He has Mrs. Brook time too but Mrs. Brook says it's good for everyone to be in a regular class. But he screams a lot so I'm glad he's not in my class except for recess and PE. Now he's screaming LOUD and the lady who helps him tries to get him up but William H. is kicking too much.

Josh has a big grinny smile on his face. You shouldn't smile when you do something bad because a smile is supposed to mean you're being nice. I wish people would follow the Facial Expressions Chart like they're supposed to.

The lady who helps William H. talks to Josh. Her hands are on her hips and her head is moving up and down and she keeps leaning forward and back again. I think this means she's mad. Sometimes it means The Chicken Dance but I don't think that's what she's doing right now. Finally she walks away and Josh shrugs. This means he doesn't Get It. I decide to be helpful because that's something I'm good at so I go over to Josh.

Ew! he yells. *You're like a dog! Slobbering all over your sleeve!*

I stop sucking my sleeve even though I don't know why he says *Ew*. I like dogs. Dogs sit next to you and put their chin on your lap. Dogs are sweet and kind. I'm happy if people think I'm a dog.

What do you want? Freak! Josh says, and I remember why I'm there.

You shouldn't get in someone's Personal Space.

What's it to you?

I don't know what that means so I say again, *You shouldn't get in someone's Personal Space.*

He puts his hands on his hips and his nose wrinkles up. *What of it?*

He must mean, What IS it. *Personal Space is this.* I step right in front of him—I even step on his toes—to show him where his Personal Space is.

Get off me you freak! he yells.

You need to remember Your Manners, I tell him. *You should say, Excuse me please but you're in My Personal Space.*

His head leans forward and his mouth drops open.

I think this means confused so I tell him again. *Listen carefully. This is what you say. Excuse me please but—*

Get out of here!

I shake my head. *No. That's not the polite way to say it. You say, Excuse me—*

Why are you bugging me? he shouts.

I'm not. I'm teaching you how to say Excuse me.

I'm not going to say it!

Okay. You can say, Sorry.

I don't have to! I didn't do anything wrong!

I Look At The Person. *Yes. You. Did.* I say it slowly so maybe he'll understand.

Josh's face is red and he's breathing hard all of a sudden like he has been running even though he hasn't been. *Is this about your brother?*

Why is he talking about Devon? This conversation is about William H.

I don't have to apologize for that! That wasn't me! Okay? That was my cousin! I didn't do anything!

Your cousin is dead. Remember? YOU are the one who did something wrong, I say, because I SAW him push William H. out of his Personal Space.

I can't help it that your brother was shot!

I don't know why he's yelling at me.

It's not my fault!

I hate shouting. I'm starting to shake.

They tried to save him at the hospital! Josh yells.

I'm shaking my head now because I want him to stop.

But he doesn't. *His Heart was hanging out and they couldn't close his chest up—*

Shut up Josh! It's Emma from my class. There are a bunch of kids behind her.

31

I'm just—

Stop it! Why are you talking about this?

I suck my sleeve but I can't help moaning even though I'm not supposed to.

She brought it up! Josh says. *She's accusing me!*

Well she's upset!

Yeah, a boy says as he gives Josh a shove.

Josh practically falls into me so I step away and Josh lands on the ground. Some people laugh.

Josh stares up at me with slitty eyes. *It's not my fault her brother is DEAD!*

NOOOO! I hear a scream and only when I try to run far FAR away from it but it keeps following me do I realize that it's me.

CHAPTER 6

THE HEART

I FIND THIRTY-TWO BOOKS IN
the library about how the Heart works. Dad
talks with the librarian and says it's okay for
me to use his card too so I can check out a lot
of books. Some of them are kids' books and
some are adult books but I can read anything because my reading score is so high
they can't even rate it. When I was in kindergarten I was above eighth-grade level and that
was as far as you could get in kindergarten.

Now I'm in fifth grade which is why I can read anything Dad can.

Sometimes I read the same books over and over and over. What's great about books is that the stuff inside doesn't change. People say you can't judge a book by its cover but that's not true because it says right on the cover what's inside. And no matter how many times you read that book the words and pictures don't change. You can open and close books a million times and they stay the same. They look the same. They say the same words. The charts and pictures are the same colors.

Books are not like people. Books are safe.

The librarian won't let you take the *Physicians' Desk Reference* home even if you hide it in the middle of thirty-two books. She says you have to leave it in the reference section so others might enjoy it. I don't think I should have to leave it in the reference section just so others *might* enjoy. I know I *will* enjoy it. But she says that is not the point. She never does tell me what the point is but Devon says sometimes you just have to do what a teacher or librarian says even if you think it's stupid. Also he says you shouldn't tell them out loud that you think it's stupid. That's a secret that stays in your head only.

On the way home Dad stops at CVS and buys me a whole bag of gummy worms.

Why? I ask.

Aren't these your favorite?

Yes but I don't have ten stickers in a row yet on YOUR MANNERS chart.

Mrs. Brook says you're doing an excellent job at school considering . . . everything.

She's right! I make a smiley face with my mouth. I deserve these gummy worms because I do spend all my time considering everything. I just don't always Get It.

I eat one green gummy worm and one red. Their names are Eddie and Talia. I always name my gummy worms before I eat them. When we get home I stuff some in every pocket of my pants so I'll always have one when I need one. Then I start reading.

There's a lot of information about the Heart in thirty-two books and I read it all. Here's what I'm writing down in my Word Study notebook because these are the words I want to study more than eLIMinate and DEVastate:

CHAMbers

AORta

Atria

VENtricles

VEINS

ARteries

VALVES

I also learn that you should exercise right like Devon who plays soccer and baseball and runs almost every day. You should eat good foods like Devon who doesn't eat nearly as much candy as me. You shouldn't smoke because it can hurt your Heart and it smells so bad it makes you want to throw up. Devon never throws up but even he says that.

There are many Heart diseases. Some of them you get from smoking and drinking and being fat and not exercising. Some of them you get from an infection. Some of them you get when you're old. Some problems you're born with. Most of the diseases you can do something about like take lots of pills. Sometimes a Heart problem happens all of a sudden and there is not much you can do. But you should try to get to a hospital right away to increase your chances of survival.

What I can't find is how long you can make a Heart

work once it is shot and can other body organs take over for it and can a hospital keep you alive without it and are you the same person without it and are you a person at all?

This is all I can find on that topic:

A gunshot wound to the Heart is almost always fatal.

CHAPTER 7

GROUPS

MRS. JOHNSON FINISHES EX-
plaining our group project which can be about
any animal we choose. She asks us to give her
some choices and writes them on the board.

I choose the Heart.

Her marker squeaks to a halt on the white-
board. *I see,* she says, turning slowly to Look At
The Person. *Of what animal?*

*I don't care. As long as it's human. I'm really
good at drawing the human Heart now.*

The class laughs.

She sighs. *I want you to write about an animal. How about a panda?*

I shake my head. Can't she see I'm already drawing a Heart in my notebook?

Another animal?

I shake my head again.

Well. Think about it. Maybe you'll come up with some animals that'll interest you.

After she writes a bunch more animals on the board she says to break into groups. Everyone moves except me. Mrs. Johnson stands in front of my desk. *Would you like help finding a group?*

I have a group.

Who's in your group?

Me.

Who else?

Nobody. I'm my own group.

Someone laughs.

I'd like you to be in a real group. How about joining Emma and Brianna?

No.

More kids laugh.

Mrs. Johnson narrows her eyes and mouth at them but turns back to me. *Excuse me?*

No Thank You. That's another sticker for my YOUR MANNERS chart.

Everyone laughs now.

Mrs. Johnson takes a big breath and lets it out. *I want you to be part of a group.*

I stare at her hands.

Do you understand?

Yes. I understand what she wants but I also know what I want.

So will you come over and join them now?

She doesn't understand. I shake my head. *No.*

Why not?

I sigh and try to explain it so she'll Get It. *I know that's what you want but it's not what I want.*

Hi, says Mrs. Brook, *you're early.*

I know. I told Mrs. Johnson that but she said it was time to see you NOW. She's having trouble Getting It today.

Oh. Let's Talk About It.

I explain about the group project.

Caitlin. When a teacher says she wants you to do something that means you should do it. It's the same as saying you have to do it.

Well why didn't she say that?

It's a nice way of saying it.

No it's not. It's a confusing way of saying it. And she should say PLEASE if she's trying to be nice.

Would that have helped? If she'd said please?

Maybe. Should I share that with her?

Why don't you let me talk with her instead. And why don't you want to do a group project with some of the girls?

I can do a better group project by my own self.

I'm sure you can do a wonderful project but there's value in working with a group.

What's the value?

Making friends.

I already have friends.

Tell me about your friends.

My Dictionary. TV. Computer.

Mrs. Brook shakes her head. *I'm talking about people and learning how to get along with others.*

I know how. I leave them alone.

Not that way.

But that's what they always tell me—Leave me alone. Caitlin go away—so I'm listening. And I'm doing what they asked so I'm being nice.

Mrs. Brook's head drops down and she squeezes her hands into fists. *It can be difficult but I'm going to help you.* She Looks At The Person. *Let's think about the children in your class.*

I stare at the Facial Expressions Chart. I start stuffed-animaling it.

Are you thinking?

I already did.

Who did you think of?

I'm thinking of people who smile a lot. That's supposed to mean happy and nice and friendly. And which people have mad faces or cry a lot because that means they're sad. Or mad. Or scared.

Or sometimes even happy and just feeling emotional, Mrs. Brook says.

See! That's why emotions are evil and I hate them! Especially crying. I don't Get It.

Laughing is easier to figure out, she says. *It usually shows that you're happy.*

Not always. Sometimes it shows that you're being mean.

That's true—if someone is teasing or making fun of someone.

WHEN, I tell her, *not if.*

She sighs. *I suppose it's just as hard to figure out emotions from laughing too.*

Now I'm thinking about Josh.

Mrs. Brook does her turtle head jerk. *Oh? Do you . . . like him?*

No.

Let's try to pick someone you like and we'll work on a friendship with that person. That's the first thing to think about.

Oh. You didn't say that.

Who do you like?

I don't know.

Think hard.

Miss Harper.

Miss Harper?

Yes. She's the princiPAL. Get It? She's everyone's pal.

Yes okay but I'm thinking of someone your age.

Who are you thinking of?

No one in particular. I'd like you to think of someone.

I don't like this game. *I give up so why don't you just tell me?*

Well—how about Emma?

Emma?

Yes. She's very outgoing.

I don't like very outgoing. Or efFUSive. Or EXtroverted. Or greGARious. Or any of those words that mean their loudness fills up my ears and hurts and their face and waving arms invade my Personal Space and their constant talking sucks all the air out of the room until I think I'm going to choke.

It's easier to talk with people who are outgoing. Just think about it.

This is what I'm thinking: Mrs. Brook does not Get It.

You're a very special person Caitlin. I think you'll be a wonderful friend.

Okay maybe she does Get It. I'm the one who doesn't. She lets me look up friend in her Dictionary. It says: somebody emotionally close.

There's that evil word again. Emotionally. That is not one of my strengths.

But you can develop that strength.

I look away and suck on my sleeve. I'm not ready to develop that strength just yet.

Mrs. Brook seems to Get It. She sighs and says she'll talk with Mrs. Johnson and maybe this time I can be my own group because there's a lot going on in my life right now but soon I'll have to join the group.

I don't like the word soon because you don't know when it's going to sneak up on you and turn into NOW. Or maybe it'll be the kind of soon that never happens. Like when I asked Dad and Devon when the chest would be finished. They said soon.

CHAPTER 8

BAMBI

I'M DOING MY GROUP PROJECT on the Heart and how it works and how a gunshot wound to the Heart makes it stop working and what they do with the body when it's dead which is cremate it. At least that's what happened to Devon.

When I finish my last drawing I go to the sofa where Dad is sitting and show it to him. He reads it and his head droops almost to his knees. The bump on his throat goes in and out every time he swallows. He sniffs several times which means at least three times and actually he sniffs five times before I say, *What's wrong with it?*

Nothing, he says. *It's—it's very well done. I . . . need to go take a shower. You can pick out a video and watch it.*

Yay! And I don't even have all the stickers I need for a video! I run over to the shelf with the videos and stop. *Why are you taking a shower at night? You always take a shower in the morning.*

He is already out of the living room. *I'm a little sore . . .* and I don't hear what he says after that except he must be really sore because I hear him crying even before the shower turns on.

I don't want to hear the crying so I focus on my favorite videos. I don't like the ones the other girls at school like with loud music and girls who giggle and dance. I like cartoons. I pick up *Cinderella* but it's kind of a stupid story. Not because she lost a shoe. I lose shoes all the time. But if you know where you lost your shoe why don't you go back and get it? And if you don't know Devon always says go back to the last place you remember having it and start looking there. Cinderella should go back to the dance. *Snow White* is okay because of the dwarves and *Pocahontas* is good because of the animals but Devon says the music is crying music and Dad is already crying so I don't want that.

I pull out *Bambi* and look at it. *Bambi* reminds me how smart I am. Sometimes I'm smarter than Devon even though he is three years and one month and sixteen days older than me. Even when I was five years old and we watched *Bambi*. Bambi's mother is shot dead. You don't see her die because it's a cartoon but you hear the gun and you see Bambi call and call for his mother and she never comes back so she is definitely dead. Devon kept saying, *She can't be dead! She can't be dead,* and I said, *She's DEAD Devon!* He started crying and saying, *She's coming back! She has to come back,* so I had to yell at him, *SHE'S DEAD AND SHE'S NEVER COMING BACK,* and Dad had to come and take Devon out of the room because like Dad said, *You shouldn't say things like that!*

I don't know why Devon couldn't Get It that the mother was dead. Our mother died two years before we watched *Bambi* so he should've known that mothers die and that they don't ever come back again no matter how much you cry or call for them. Especially if they're shot dead.

I look over at Devon's chest. The air from the heat pump is making the sheet lift up just a bit. Then it stops dead. I look back at the *Bambi* video and put it back on the shelf because it's giving me a recess feeling in my stomach and I don't know why.

CHAPTER **9**

NO RUNNING.
WALKING.

WHEN I GO TO MRS. BROOK TIME
she says to go get my coat because we're switching our schedule.

Today?

She nods. *And for the rest of the year.* She
shuts her door and her shoes start squeaking
across the floor toward the coat hooks outside
my classroom.

Why? I don't like switching things. It's always recess first—yuck—then Mrs. Brook time. Her shoes keep squeaking down the hall so I have to walk-run to catch up with her because there's No Running In The Halls. *What's the schedule going to be now?*

We're going to have our time together while we walk around the playground during your regular recess. Then you can stay outside and have recess with the kindergarten through second graders.

I Look At The Person. *Two recesses? I don't even like one recess.*

But the little kids are very sweet and I'll be with you for recess with the older kids because sometimes they can be . . . She presses her lips together. I think it's a mad face. *A little rough.*

I think about Josh. And I wonder why a grown-up wants to go to recess at all. *Okay. But don't even try getting on the monkey bars. It's too dangerous.*

Mrs. Brook smiles. *I promise you I'll avoid the monkey bars.*

I take my jacket from the hook and put it on as Mrs. Brook pushes the bar on the door to the playground and it clanks open. The brightness outside hurts my eyes and the wind makes them water and the screaming on the playground stabs my ears. I suck my sleeve and walk fast to try to get away from it even though it follows me everywhere.

Caitlin! What are you doing so far ahead of me?

I'm walking. And you're slow.

Usually when two people go for a walk together, Mrs. Brook says, *they actually walk together.*

Oh, I say, and keep walking.

Caitlin! Walk back to me. Please.

So I walk backward to her and stop. *Now what?*

Let's walk next to each other. That's what going for a walk together means. She puts her right foot out first then her left.

I do the exact same thing.

You don't need to stare at my feet, she says. *And you don't need to match my exact stride or use your left foot when I use mine.*

Then how is that walking together? I ask.

We're going to keep pace with each other because we're talking to each other while we walk. Sometimes we'll make eye contact too. That lets the other person know that we're listening and interested.

What if we're not interested?

She Looks At The Person and she opens her eyes wide and she speaks slowly. *We're going to act like we're interested. Okay? We'll use this time to observe people and maybe talk to them. We really need to work hard on making friends.*

Why? I ask. *Don't you have any? Recess isn't the best place to make friends.*

I want to work on friendships for YOU. You'll be going to the middle school soon and I want you to have some friends there.

Middle school is sixth grade, I remind her. *That's next year.*

Actually you only have a few months left in elementary school. Sixth grade starts in August.

She's right. Why does everyone say next year? It's not next year. It's this year. I suck on my sleeve some more even though I know Mrs. Brook doesn't like me to.

There'll be more group projects in middle school so you'll have to learn to Deal With That. Having friends will help.

Can't I Deal With It by being my own group?

Mrs. Brook shakes her head. This means no.

I keep sucking my sleeve.

Caitlin. Why don't you try clasping your hands together or putting your hands in your pockets and squeezing them into fists or one of the other things we've talked about instead of sucking your sleeve?

I stop sucking my sleeve but I'll go back to it later when she forgets because I'm persistent.

She nods at kids on the playground and tells me what they're doing and how they're feeling but I don't know how she can tell. I don't even know which kids she's talking about. They all move around too fast. When she mentions the boy in the purple hooded sweatshirt I try to keep up with him and I wish I had a purple sweatshirt like that because purple is my favorite color and I think I might like a hood and it's fun to watch the flying purple when he runs really fast.

Caitlin!

What?

You're far ahead of me again. We're supposed to be keeping pace with each other so we can talk.

Oh. I thought you were done talking.

Look in my eyes while we walk and talk. That will help you keep pace.

I keep switching my eyes away to give them a break but she keeps catching me.

Finally she says, *There. That's much better.*

Except that my eyes hurt and my neck is stiff. How is that better?

When the bell rings Mrs. Brook tells me I have twenty minutes of recess with the little kids and then I have to go back to my classroom like they do. *If you have any trouble go see one of the teachers.*

Inside?

No. There are always at least three teachers on recess duty out here.

Really? I never see any teachers outside at big kid recess.

We always have several outside but they're kept quite busy because there are a lot of kids on the playground at the same time.

I know. Too many. It's way too loud.

CHAPTER 10

MICHAEL AND MANNERS

IT'S LOUD AT LITTLE KID RECESS too but I like these kids much better. They don't hurt as much when they run into you. They're my size or smaller. I look around and smile.

I see a little boy in a red baseball cap that reminds me of Devon's red Potomac Nationals baseball cap. And I remember seeing that boy at the memorial service for Devon because I remember that cap. He was sitting hunched over on a pew just the way he's sitting hunched over on a bench right now. I wonder why he's sitting like that. There's no teacher next to him so I don't think he's in trouble. He's rubbing his eyes so he's either sleepy or sad. I think those are the only two things it could be.

I walk closer to see if I can figure out which it is. He looks up when I'm near and I can see his reddish wet face.

Are you sad?

He nods.

Why?

He doesn't say anything.

I look around for Josh but then remember that he's not out at this recess. *Is someone else being mean to you?*

He shakes his head.

I put my hands in my pants pocket and rediscover my gummy worms. I pull one out and dangle it in front of him. *Want this? Her name is Laurie.*

He looks at it for a moment then takes it but doesn't put it in his mouth.

It's not a real worm, I tell him. *It's to eat.*

He still doesn't eat it and I'm about to ask him to give it back if he's not going to eat it but then he says, *Thank you.* I don't think I can take it back now.

He puts it in his mouth and part of it hangs out as he chews. Finally the worm disappears. *I miss her,* he says.

Laurie the worm?

He shakes his head. *Mommy.*

Oh.

He turns his head to look up at me and moves closer but doesn't invade my Personal Space. I try to look in his eyes. When I do I'm surprised. They are like Bambi eyes. They're simple. Like the eyes on the Facial Expressions Chart and they stay still so I can see what's inside.

Don't you miss your brother? he asks. The Bambi eyes do not even blink.

What do you mean?

He's dead. Right?

How do you know?

Everyone says you're the weirdo whose brother is dead. Oh. Sorry. I didn't mean to say weirdo. That's just what people say. Are you weird?

I don't know.

He shrugs. *You're not weird to me. I think you're nice.*

Thank you, I say. I'm remembering Your Manners.

I hear someone clap. A teacher voice calls out, *Okay class! Two minutes! Then we need to line up!*

Thanks for the gummy worm.

Very good, I say, *you remembered Your Manners.*

He nods. *Mommy said that's important.*

It is. You get stickers.

His lips go down a little at the ends and his head tilts like he doesn't Get It. *I don't think that's why.*

You do get a sticker though, I tell him.

From who?

Your dad.

He doesn't have any stickers.

I have a lot. I can bring you some.

Okay. Thanks.

You said thanks. That's two stickers now. You're welcome. See? I'm good at Your Manners too.

He giggles. *They're not MY manners.*

I know. They're YOUR Manners.

What? His Bambi eyes look smiley but also a little . . . something else . . . maybe confused?

Everyone has to learn Your Manners, I explain.

You're silly! He giggles some more.

Why are you laughing?

Because they're EVERYONE'S Manners! MY Manners are when I say please and thank you. YOUR Manners are when YOU say please and thank you.

I Look At The Person. All this time I thought I was learning YOUR Manners when really I was learning MY Manners? *But then . . . everyone's manners are the same.*

Now you Get It!

Ohhh. Thank you. You're very helpful. I think it'll be easier to learn YOUR Manners—I mean MY Manners—now that I know they belong to me and I'm not trying to learn somebody else's.

The bell rings and the boy stands up and looks at me with his Bambi eyes. A teacher voice calls out and he turns and starts walking toward it but then he turns around again. *What's your name?*

CaitlinAnnSmith.

Oh. Can I just call you Caitlin?

Only if you don't shout it. I hate when people shout my name.

He nods. *Okay. My name's Michael.*

I hold my right hand up and close and open it three times.

His mouth corners go up and his cheeks get puffy and his Bambi eyes smile. He has cute little dimples and blond wavy hair that drops below his cap. He holds his left hand up and opens and closes it several times back to me.

I wonder if this means I have a friend.

CHAPTER **11**

THE DAY OUR LIFE
FELL APART

MRS. JOHNSON GIVES ME BACK MY group project. It says *Well Researched* and *Very Interesting* and *Excellent* but at the bottom she also writes, *Why are there capital letters in the middle of your sentences? Common nouns are not capitalized. Only the special words are capitalized.* I look at my paragraph. I did not put capital letters in the middle of the sentences. They are only at the beginning of some words. She has put an X over the H in Heart and written a lowercase h. It doesn't look right that way. I'm sure she's wrong about the special words and capital letters even though she's a teacher. How can any word be more special than Heart?

At home I think about Devon's Heart. I sit on the sofa and look at his chest. It's still under the gray sheet. There are rays of light coming in through the blinds and the dust swirls around in the beams and hits the chest and I wonder if any of the dust particles are Devon and if I can feel him.

I close my eyes and remember some of the things that happened on The Day Our Life Fell Apart. That's what Dad calls it. After we came home from the hospital that night—with no Devon—Dad was yelling and kicking the furniture and the walls and he started pounding the chest with his fists and shouting, *Why? Why? WHY?* and he threw the woodworking books and Scout manual into Devon's room and slammed the door and said, *No no no no no,* until I screamed at him to *STOP IT! STOP IT! STOP IT!* Then he put the sheet over the chest and now he never even looks in that corner.

I press myself against the sofa and squish my eyes tight and even though I try not to I remember being at the hospital and how there were sharp lights and siren noises and loudspeaker noises and beeping noises and medicine smells and finally people dressed in green pajamas and paper slippers said to Dad, *We tried but we couldn't close your son's chest. His Heart—there was nothing left—there was nothing we could do. Nothing we could do.*

I'm shaking and sucking my sleeve and I try to stop thinking about The Day Our Life Fell Apart but when I open my eyes Devon's chest is staring at me so I slide off of the sofa and crawl over to it and pull the sheet up from the bottom and push underneath it and get inside the empty hollow chest and I imagine myself as the Heart. Devon's Heart. My arms are atria and my legs are ventricles and I pump the blood all around the right way because there *has* to be something I can do. Something I can do. First I pump the blood to the lungs to pick up the oxygen then to the left atrium and ventricle then to the aorta to go all around his body like it should. All my valves are working so the blood flow is right and I can feel the beat and I rock with it because rocking makes me feel alive and I want his chest to be alive. I pump the blood around Devon's body. *Dev-on. Dev-on. Dev-on.* I say it louder and louder to make it true and my whole body is beating for his louder and louder and wilder and wilder and my head is banging the sides of the chest but I don't care. *DEV-ON! DEV-ON! DEV-ON!* And I hear Dad's voice screaming like at the hospital and I don't want to hear it because I don't want any part of The Day Our Life Fell Apart to happen again so I focus and become the Heart louder and louder and harder and harder but then I fall out of the chest because there's no way to close it and I feel Dad grabbing me but all I can do is scream the words from the green hospital people, *I TRIED BUT THERE WAS NOTHING I COULD DO!*

Caitlin! Caitlin! I hear Dad yelling but I can't stop crying. I feel him wrap me in my blanket and put me back on the sofa and I feel his arm around me as he sits next to me in the dark. The ringing in my ears finally stops but then the phone rings.

I feel Dad get up and watch him disappear into the kitchen. He comes running back into the living room and turns on the TV and stands there looking at it. He breathes heavily.

The man on Fox Five News has a microphone in his hand and is talking in front of a brick building. *I'm at the courthouse where the remaining killer from the Virginia Dare Middle School shooting has just had his preliminary hearing. The hearing found that there's enough evidence against him to be put on trial for the murders of teacher Roberta Schneider and young students Julieanne Morris and Devon Smith. That horrific shooting was a devastating blow to this small community—oh! There he is!* The picture jumps around wildly until it's on a boy in an orange suit with police all around him. He doesn't look much older than Devon. Mr. Fox Five News shouts as he pushes his microphone past a crowd of people, *What do you have to say for yourself?* The boy in orange stares into the camera and grins a half smile. Then he lifts his handcuffed hands and gives a thumbs-up sign. Dad goes to the bathroom and throws up. The camera switches to a lady sitting inside at the news desk. She says, *We'll hear more about this story later but isn't it good that we now have closure?*

I suck my sleeve. I don't think there is anything good about any of it. And I wonder how CLOsure can help. And what it is. When Dad comes back to the living room and turns off the TV I ask him, *What is CLOsure?* He says he has to call a neighbor but when Mrs. Robbins comes over he forgets to ask her what closure means. He just says she is going to take care of me because he has a headache and needs to take a shower. I wonder if it is one of the crying showers. I close my eyes.

I can see the light come on through my eyelids and I hear a creaking sound and then Mrs. Robbins's shaky voice. *Can I get you something Caitlin? Hot chocolate? Warm milk?*

My Dictionary.

Dictionary?

Yes.

Oh. I was thinking of—

PLEASE.

More creaking. *Okay dear.*

I look up CLOsure and it says: *the state of experiencing an emotional conclusion to a difficult life event such as the death of loved one.* I do not know how to get to the state of experiencing an emotional conclusion so I ask Mrs. Robbins, *How do I get to the state of experiencing an emotional conclusion to a difficult life event?*

Her mouth opens and closes three times and makes a squeaky noise. *Excuse me,* she says, and runs into the kitchen but I can hear her blowing her nose and now I can hear Dad crying in the shower so I put my purple fleece over my head and close my eyes and plug my ears and with my elbows I squeeze my Dictionary tight against my chest.

CHAPTER **12**

CLOSURE

I WAIT ALL MORNING FOR MY MRS. Brook time. I run-walk to her room because of No Running In The Halls. I push the door open without even knocking and ask, *How do I get to the state of experiencing an emotional conclusion to a difficult life event?*

She stands up from the round table. *What do you mean?*

Closure, I say. *I'm talking about Closure. How do I find it?*

Sit down Caitlin. Is this . . . are you talking about the news? The boy from the shooting?

I nod about a hundred times because she is a little slow Getting It today.

This is very stressful for our entire community. We're all looking for Closure.

I Look At The Person. But she's not answering my question.

Come sit down.

I'm still standing.

Okay, says Mrs. Brook, *I'll sit.* She puts her hands in front of her on the table and clasps them together. She takes a deep breath and lets it out. Slowly. She closes her eyes.

Is she praying? *This isn't church,* I remind her.

I know. I'm thinking. She scratches the part in her hair then puts her hands together again. *Sometimes the process of a funeral and burial and doing things like putting wreaths on grave sites help give Closure.*

Devon was cremated so that will not work for me.

Some people go to church.

It's not Sunday, I point out.

I mean on Sundays do you and your father go to church?

I shrug. *We used to go to one with the Boy Scouts but not anymore. Now we just drive past it.*

Church might be helpful. Or seeing a counselor.

I Look At The Person. *You're a counselor. I see you.*

I know but your dad might like to go see a counselor too.

Can he come see you about Closure?

Sometimes we can do that but I'm really here to help the students. But talking can help both of you a lot, she says. *Talking about your feelings.*

That will not work for me. I don't like Let's Talk About It. Now Caitlin—

Is there anything else?

Well if nothing else, Mrs. Brook says, *time helps.*

But I didn't ask if there was nothing else. I asked if there was anything else. I start shaking my hands because the world is spinning and if I shake my hands faster than the rest of the world then the world's spinning doesn't seem so fast. Devon says it makes no sense but it makes sense to me.

It's something you have to find for yourself because everyone is different. We all have to find our own special way.

I thought I was the one who was special and everyone else was normal. I almost ask her what normal people do but I suppose that would not work for me anyway. *That doesn't help.*

She touches my shaking hand and I pull it away. *Something will come to you Caitlin,* she says. *There's a solution out there with your name written on it.*

I look around her room for my name.

I'm sorry, she says, *I don't mean that your name will actually be written on anything. But you'll think of something.*

I give a big sigh and say, *Fine. I will figure it out myself.*

But I have no clue how.

We walk together on the playground and Mrs. Brook talks but I can't hear her. I'm thinking too hard about Closure. When the bell rings I stand there sucking my sleeve until I remember I have a maybe friend and I go find Michael. He's on the jungle gym but comes over to me when I do our wave.

Hi Caitlin.

Do you know how to get to the state of experiencing an emotional conclusion to a difficult life event?

What?

Closure. Do you know how to get there?

72

No. But I'll ask my dad. He's good at finding stuff.

Really? My dad isn't. Is your dad extra smart or something?

He shrugs. *I don't know. He seems extra happy.*

You're lucky. My dad's sad all the time.

Michael shakes his head. *I don't feel lucky. I feel bad because I'm not happy all the time like he is. Like I'm supposed to be. He always wants to do something like throw a football or play Frisbee or go bowling and sometimes I just don't want to do that stuff because I'm sad.*

Maybe my dad and your dad should get together and become normal.

Maybe.

So will you ask him?

Ask him what?

About Closure?

That's a hard word.

It's like closing. Only it's Closure.

Okay. I'll ask him.

Thank you. I smile. *That's MY manners. And that reminds me. Here are YOUR stickers. They're of the planets. Some of them glow in the dark.*

He looks at the stickers. *Whoa. I LOVE these! Thank you Caitlin!*

You're welcome.

When Dad drives me home from school I look at the sign in front of the church we used to go to. It says, *OUR HEARTS are still with the families of Julianne, Devon and Roberta.* Except *OUR HEARTS* couldn't do anything to save Devon's Heart. Maybe that's why Dad drives past.

I need to figure out Closure.

CHAPTER **13**

TO KILL A MOCKINGBIRD

I'M STANDING IN FRONT OF Devon's door. Whenever I don't know what to do I go to Devon's room and ask him. I REALLY want to know about Closure. And I don't know who else to ask.

Except Devon's not here.

But his room is.

I haven't been inside since Dad slammed

the door on The Day Our Life Fell Apart. I know that means Dad doesn't want me to go in but I don't know why. Even though the door doesn't have my name on it I want to be with Devon. I need to be with Devon. And I know Devon would open his door for me.

I put my hand on the doorknob. It's cool and strong. I hold it awhile like I'm holding Devon's hand. Like I did when I followed him into his room and he let me draw while he did his homework as long as I didn't talk or hum or make weird mouth noises. I close my eyes and promise the door that I will not talk or hum or make weird mouth noises and I turn the knob. After a cracking sound the door opens.

When I push my head into the soft blue blur of his room I can smell him and feel him and I smile. It's like pure Devon in here. I go all the way in and quietly shut the door behind me.

There is the beanbag chair where Devon always sits. And the books on the floor that Dad threw there. And the bed which is never made because Devon hates making his bed. And the shelf with his trophies. Baseball. Basketball. Boy Scouts.

I look around the walls that are full of my pictures. He still has stuff taped up that I did in preschool. I don't know why. They're really bad. I can do so much better now. The bird I drew when I was four hardly even looks like a bird. Now I can draw a bird that looks real. Last year Dad entered the eagle I drew in a grown-up art show and it won first prize. Dad and Devon were so happy I was sure they got confused and thought they'd drawn the bird themselves. But they didn't because Devon said, *You may be the best artist in Virginia,* and Dad said so too.

Devon even said that by the time I'm an adult I might be the best artist in the country! I remember where he was sitting when he said it. Right there. In the blue beanbag chair with the plastic cover that feels weird and makes fart noises when you slide into it. It's Devon's favorite place to sit. Not mine.

I turn around and I see it. My hidey-hole. The best place in the world. If there's a thunderstorm or fireworks or a lot of sirens Devon lets me sit in the hidey-hole in the corner between the foot of his bed and his dresser. He even used his Boy Scout knife to carve my name underneath his dresser where Dad can't see it and get mad because you're not supposed to use stickers on the furniture and Devon says it's a pretty safe bet that the No Stickers On The Furniture rule applies to knives also.

I decide to get in my hidey-hole and slide all the way underneath the dresser and look up at my name and feel it. It's not my real name. It's Devon's name for me which is Scout. It's from *To Kill a Mockingbird* because he loves that movie. It has two kids in it: Jem and Scout. They are a brother and a sister and there is a father too and a lady I used to think was the mother who is always in the kitchen except when she leaves every night to go take care of her other children. I thought maybe that's where my mother went. To take care of her other children. And she had trouble with directions like me and couldn't find the way back here again. I asked Devon about it and he said that was crazy and I shouldn't blame Mom for having cancer and dying. She didn't want to die. I said Scout and Jem should be nicer to their mom because she is probably dying of cancer and one day will not be able to come back and fix them breakfast. He said, *She's a maid!* but she still seems like a mom to me.

The dad has funny glasses and is always dressed up and doesn't get mad even when people spit in his face. I wish Dad wouldn't shout when I throw things at him. And he shot a dog. Jem and Scout's dad I mean. But Devon said it was a sick dog who would attack them and make them all die. I guess sometimes it's good to shoot things. But not Devon. Devon was not going to attack anyone or make them die.

Devon is like Jem. A lot like Jem. He even looks like Jem. Except Devon's nose got broken playing baseball. And I don't know what color Jem's hair or eyes actually are because the movie is in black and white which means mostly gray. Devon's hair is brown and people say his eyes are big and beautiful and brown but really there's a lot of black and white in his eyes. I like things in black and white. Black and white is easier to understand. All that color is too confusing.

I look a little like Scout. I looked more like Scout when I was seven and Devon cut my hair like hers except Dad said not to do that ever ever again. I didn't mind the haircut. I would not like to wear a ham costume like Scout had to in the movie however but if I did I know Devon would take care of me like Jem did even if someone tried to stop him with a knife like the bad guy in the movie. I wonder if Devon was trying to help someone like me when the bad guy with the bullet stopped him.

The first time we watched *To Kill a Mockingbird* I waited through the whole movie for the dad to shoot a mockingbird. He'd already shot a dog. And he was a good shot. No one shot a bird for the whole entire movie. At the end I said it was the stupidest name ever for a movie. Devon said I didn't know what I was talking about. This year he read it in English and he said the title makes perfect sense and this is what it means:

It's wrong to shoot someone who is innocent and was never going to hurt you in the first place.

I still didn't Get It and said, *But you told me the dog was sick and he WAS going to hurt them.*

And Devon said, *It's not about the dog! It's about people! You shouldn't hurt innocent people Scout. That's what it means.*

I guess the evil school shooters didn't listen in English class because they did not Get the meaning of that book at all.

CHAPTER **14**

MY SKILLS

WE ARE AT RECESS AND I THINK
Mrs. Brook might have Asperger's too because
she is very persistent which is one of my skills.
She is stuck on her Let's Make Friends idea
even though I am making it very clear with my
eyes that I am no longer interested in this conversation. All I want to talk about is Closure
because even though I got to be in my hidey-
hole again I still didn't find Closure. All Mrs.
Brook talks about is the many ways to make

friends. I suck on my sleeve but she says that's not one of them.

Friends give comfort to each other. Friends help solve problems. You can share so much with friends, she says in her Nice Voice.

Like gummy worms? I feel in my pocket and I have three worms.

I was thinking more like feelings.

Oh. I don't have any of those.

Of course you do. But if you're not interested in sharing feelings you can share some thoughts and ideas.

I think about how much people might laugh at me if I shared thoughts and ideas. *Why?*

These are all interpersonal skills that help you deal with people.

Interpersonal skills are not part of my skill set. Remember?

Tell me what's in your skill set.

I can belch my ABCs.

I'm not sure girls your age would really appreciate that.

Oh. How about the boys?

More likely. Let's hear some of your other skills though.

I sigh. *Do you want to hear the whole list?*

Yes.

I sigh again. *It's long.*

We have time.

Fine. I tell her my list and make my head go back and forth like a *ticktock* of the clock.

Drawing. Tick.

Memorizing stuff. Tock.

Remembering stuff other people forget. Tick.

Looking stuff up in books and the computer. Tock.

Being helpful. Tick.

Hearing stuff that other people can't. Tock.

Being nice. Tick.

Being honest. Tock.

Reading. Tick.

Fixing cereal the right way. Tock.

Seeing stuff that other people don't see. Tick.

Loading the dishwasher. Tock.

Being persistent. I Look At The Person. *Like I want Closure NOT friends.* Tick.

Mrs. Brook is all excited about my list and tells me how to share my skills with other people. I don't really listen because she didn't listen to my hint about Closure.

After a while I hear her voice again. *Caitlin. Let's observe the interpersonal skills that are going on around us right now.*

How?

See those two girls over there by the swings?

I squint where she's pointing.

One of them is comforting the other who must be sad or hurt.

Which is which?

Mrs. Brook's head does its turtle jerk. *The girl in the red jacket has her arm around the girl in jeans. Right?*

Yes.

So she's comforting the girl in the jeans.

Oh. How can she tell that so fast and easily? It must be why she's a counselor.

We watch some other interpersonal skills on the playground. One boy kicks a stone. Mrs. Brook says he is angry because obviously he wanted to tag everyone out but didn't. I don't think it's obvious at all. I think it's dangerous to kick a stone though. Mrs. Brook says it's okay to do it just once and look how quickly he rejoined the game isn't that nice?

She makes me start guessing what people are thinking

which is a stupid game because how am I supposed to know what's going on inside their heads?

She points to some girls who are standing in a circle talking and giggling LOUD. They are bent. *What do you think they're feeling?*

Like throwing up?

She Looks At The Person.

Well they're bending over so much it looks like they're going to throw up.

Do you usually laugh a lot just before you throw up?

No. I don't. But who knows about them?

Do you really think that's what they're about to do?

I have no idea. I'm not them.

But if you put yourself in their shoes you can feel what they're feeling.

I look at their shoes.

It's an expression, she says. *What we're working on Caitlin is empathy.*

Is that like emotion?

Sort of.

No thank you. I'm not good with emotion.

All you need to do is imagine how other people are feeling.

Why?

Then you know how to communicate with them.

What if I don't want to? Or can't.

Listen Caitlin. This is important. If they're happy you can be happy with them. If someone is very sad you should be quiet with them and maybe try to cheer them up a little bit but not start out all loud and happy because that doesn't match their emotion.

You're not matching my emotion right now.

Oh? What emotion are you feeling right now?

Kind of annoyed. And bored.

She is quiet for a moment. *That's more of an attitude than an emotion. Underneath the attitude how are you feeling?*

Okay I guess.

Happy?

I don't know. Maybe confused.

She nods. *This is difficult. Understanding people and finding friends isn't easy for anyone.*

It's harder for me.

Yes it is.

Isn't there an easier way to make friends?

You can look for children who are by themselves and might like a friend to play with.

I shake my head. *There aren't any people by themselves. They all have friends.*

They might like to have another friend. And I bet they don't all have friends. Haven't you ever seen someone standing alone?

I shrug. *Just one.*

Why don't you talk to that child?

Because it's me and Devon told me I shouldn't talk to myself. Not in public anyway.

I think you're just not seeing them. You have to look at people very carefully.

I'm not good at that.

You need to practice.

I shake my head.

Why not?

That's a LOT of work.

You can try a little bit at a time.

I sigh.

For example. Look at me.

I do.

Not that way. Look in my eyes.

I sigh and fold my arms. *Fine.* I glance at her eyes. They

87

are black and white and brown. Like Devon's. I never noticed that before. I'm so surprised that I actually stare instead of looking away.

*Good! That's very good Caitlin! That's how you show peo-
ple you're interested in them and that you're listening to them.
Can you see how happy my eyes are right now?*

I nod. I'm still staring at her eyes or where her eyes used
to be when she turns her head to look where she's walking.
When she turns back I catch the eyes again and keep staring. I'm getting good at this.

*Okay but you don't have to stare quite so hard or quite so
long.*

I close my eyes.

*You can just look away briefly and then come back to my
eyes again.*

I do.

*Try to make it a little smoother so you don't look like you're
about to jump on top of me when you stare into my eyes.*

See? It's too hard!

*But you did it! All we're doing now is working on refine-
ment. You just have to keep trying. It's all about finesse.*

Fin-NESS?

Yes.

I like that word. What does it mean?

Doing something tactfully and skillfully while dealing with a difficult situation.

I'm surprised that I'm only learning this word now. This word is all about me! It's what I'm trying to do every day to Deal With this difficult situation called life.

CHAPTER 15

FINESSE

I STILL HAVEN'T FOUND CLO-
sure and I remember that Michael was going
to ask his dad. When it's time for Mrs. Brook
to leave I run around the playground looking
for him.

Finally I see his red baseball cap over by the
slide and run up behind him. *Did you ask your
dad about Closure?*

He turns around. *Hi Caitlin!*

Did you ask your dad about Closure?

Yup.

What did he say?

Let's play football.

I don't like football.

No. I mean that's what my dad said.

What does that have to do with Closure?

I don't know. That's how he answers a lot of questions.

Oh. Sometimes grown-ups don't answer questions.

What's Closure anyway?

It helps you feel better after someone dies.

Oh. Can I have some?

No because I don't have any and I don't know how to get it.

His head droops down. I think this means sad.

But I'm going to find it.

Will you share it with me?

Okay.

He Looks At The Person. His eyes are soft and squishy.
Promise?

I nod.

Scout's honor?

I Look At The Person too. Hard. How does he know my
nickname?

Scout's honor? he asks again.

I nod. *Scout's honor.*

That's when I notice that Michael is wearing overalls. Just like the ones Scout wears in *To Kill a Mockingbird.*

Hey! Those are what you wear in To Kill a Mockingbird!

He frowns. *I don't kill any birds.* Michael is very smart for such a little kid.

That's good, I tell him, *because you shouldn't.*

Then why did you say it?

It's what Scout wears in To Kill a Mockingbird. *It's a movie.*

Ohhh.

I stare at his overalls. *What do they feel like?*

He looks down at his chest then rubs his hand across the pocket. *Sort of like jeans. You can feel them if you want.* He sticks his chest out toward me.

I shake my head. *I was wondering if the straps hurt or if the waist part is too loose and gets airy and cold.*

He shrugs. *They feel okay to me.* He puts his hand behind his neck. *I don't like this sweatshirt though. It's got a sticky-outy tag.*

I hate those! I tell Michael. *You should get the ones that don't have any tags. That's what I get.*

Dad bought me some new clothes but he isn't very good at it. Not like my mom.

You just have to tell him what you want. I wear sweatpants and a long-sleeved T-shirt every day. Except in summer. Then my sweatpants and T-shirts are short sleeved. The T-shirt can be any color. I don't care as long as it's not yellow or gold or mossy green or pukey green or poopy green—That makes Michael start giggling—*or any kind of pink because those colors make me feel sick. And it can only be one color because I don't like colors running into each other. And there can't be writing on the T-shirt or people will read it and I don't want them looking at me. And the long-sleeve T-shirts can't have scratchy cuffs. And none of the T-shirts can have tags in the back or collars. Or stripes. Or pockets. Or zigzag stitching. Or double stitching. Now my dad knows and he says I'm such a breeze to buy for.*

Michael giggles again.

I smile just like I do when Dad says it because even though I don't know what he means exactly I do know that breezes are nice so it must be good.

Then I notice Michael's face. *Have you been eating dirt,* I ask him.

He frowns and shakes his head. *Only William H. eats dirt.*

93

I know. So what's that brown stuff on your face?

He puts his hand on his face and rubs it around then looks at his fingers. *Frosting!* He grins and licks his fingers. *From the birthday cupcakes.*

Is it your birthday?

No. It's Shauna's. My birthday is in October. I think. Or it's November. Which one has Halloween in it?

October. That's my favorite holiday.

Mine too! Except for my birthday. I'll be seven! That's old.

I'm about to tell him that seven is still a baby but then I remember about finesse so all I say is, *I'll be eleven next month.*

Wow! You're really old! You must know a lot of stuff.

I do. But some stuff I just learned about. Like finesse.

What's that?

It's hard to explain but it's something I have a lot of.

Oh.

Do you want me to burp my ABCs? I ask him.

Can you do that?

I nod.

Do it! Do it!

So I do and he stares at me with his mouth open until I

get to XYZ and then he falls on the ground giggling. *Can I get my friends and you do it for them?*

Is Josh one of your friends?

He shakes his head as I remember that it's second recess so Josh is already inside.

Okay. Sure.

I watch and see how he gets his friends. He touches them but doesn't grab. He Looks At The Person but he doesn't get in their Personal Space. He also calls out to some of his friends who are playing and pulls his hands toward his chest several times. Then he points at me and starts running toward me. And it's like his friends are tied to him with string because they run to him from all directions until they all end up in front of me.

This is my friend Caitlin, Michael says.

I feel proud to hear him say that.

She can burp her ABCs!

No way!

Really?

You can?

Do it!

And I do. They think I am awesome. And we make

other noises and roll our tongues and cross our eyes and wiggle our ears and hop in a circle and before I know it the bell rings and they all run to the teacher.

I feel like Snow White because now I have a bunch of little dwarf friends who love me. I may not know how Scout's overalls feel but I think I know how Snow White's shoes feel because now I know why Snow White was happy.

CHAPTER **16**

THE LIST

I'M BACK IN DEVON'S ROOM staring up at SCOUT carved into the wood and seeing my special name makes me feel good. Devon said his favorite part in *To Kill a Mockingbird* is where Scout talks to the crowd of angry men and makes them go away. All she says is hi and that she knows their kids from school. Then all the angry men leave. I don't Get It. But Devon says that's exactly what I'm like because I say stuff that's obvious and people go, *Oh,* and it makes them think. He says I can solve a lot of problems just by being like Scout. Except I haven't found Closure. I wonder if I'm more like Scout will I be able to find Closure? Dad said no about the Scout haircut but maybe I could dress like Scout. I suck on my sleeve and wonder if I could wear Scout overalls like Michael. I wonder what Devon would say about Scout overalls?

After a while I decide to get my Dictionary even though I've looked up Closure thirty-seven times and it still doesn't help. I crawl out of my hidey-hole to go to my room and I see the woodworking books on the floor and read them instead. I see new words that sound cool like dado and kerf and tenon and mortise. I finish the three woodworking books which are pretty short and the Scout manual. I look under Devon's comforter that's on the floor to see if there are any other books. There aren't. But there's a piece of spiral notebook paper with Devon's handwriting.

It says *EAGLE SCOUT PROJECT* on top.

Underneath it says, *Mission-style chest with two shelves and one door.*

Then there's a list:

Quarter-cut oak
Circular saw or table saw
Plane
Router
Saber saw
Drill
Bar clamps or pipe clamps
Woodworker's glue
Sander
Wood screws
Hinges
Tack cloth
Wipe-on polyurethane varnish
Protective eyeglasses and ear protection

And at the very bottom it says this:

*Practice teaching woodworking steps to Scout. Once
she gets it, set up meeting to teach troop.*

I stare at the paper. He was going to teach me woodworking. And I realize that he taught me everything I know

and now I may never Get anything ever again because he's not here to teach me.

I don't feel good in this room anymore so I go get my purple fleece and wrap it around me and go to the living room. I get partly under the sofa cushion but leave an opening so I can stare out at Devon's chest.

Dad sits down on the floor next to me. I can see his work pants and boots. *Are you okay?*

I stare at the chest.

He sighs. His hands drop onto his legs and he sighs again. *Listen. Caitlin. It'll be your birthday before long. What would you like to do?*

Last year Devon took me to the mall. Limited Too. He said I need to wear clothes that don't make me look weird. He told me which clothes they were. I didn't like the first seventeen tops he picked.

The first one was pink. Pink is the color of medicine and feels drippy and sicky.

The second one had a tag that itched.

The third one felt like carnivorous dinosaur skin and I would be eaten alive.

The fourth one had a stripe at an angle and was evil.

It's not evil, Devon said.

It's evil, evil, evil! I said, and I screamed until he put his hand over my mouth and I bit his finger hard and he tried to get his finger out of my mouth but I wouldn't let him until I saw the tears coming out of his eyes. He crumpled on the floor holding his finger tight and his face went red and I realized for the first time that Devon feels pain.

And now I wonder if he felt pain on The Day Our Life Fell Apart?

I feel a cold hand on my arm and I flinch. It's Dad. *Caitlin. What do you want to do for your birthday?*

I whisper that I want Devon to take me to the mall.

Dad moves around so his head is peeking in at me. *What?*

I want Devon to take me shopping like he did last year.

Dad puts his head down so his chin touches his chest. He says nothing for a while. Then he looks up. *He can't.*

But it's MY birthday and that's what I want.

He sighs and explains that Devon is no longer with us and is in Heaven with my mother and the two of them are looking down on us and will always love us.

I know that. Why is he explaining it all? Is he reminding himself?

When he finally finishes I say, *I still want him to take me.*

Dad shakes his head and he stares at the carpet but his eyes are watery. Maybe he's stuffed-animaling. Finally he says he will get dinner started. This means the conversation is over.

I push my head farther under the sofa cushion but it doesn't swallow me up like I want it to.

CHAPTER **17**

KEEP YOUR PANTS ON

I'M DOING MUCH BETTER AT keeping pace with Mrs. Brook at recess. She says I don't look like I'm marching in step anymore so it's much more natural AND she says that shows a lot of finesse. I smile until she says the next thing.

Your dad is worried that you might not understand that Devon . . . isn't alive. He tells me you say, Devon says this or Devon does that, as if he's still alive.

I do say that but it doesn't mean I think he's still alive. He was alive when he said those things though.

Your dad said you want Devon to take you shopping.

I do.

But Devon can't take you shopping. Do you understand that?

Yes. But he asked what I want. That's what I want. I know I can't have it.

I see. When you're talking with your dad about Devon you might want to make it clear that you understand he's now gone.

Will that make Dad happy?

I think so. Yes.

Fine. I'll try.

Mrs. Brook smiles. *You know what? You're starting to show empathy.*

I am?

You feel for your dad. You know he's hurting and you want to make him happy. That's wonderful.

I nod even though I'm not sure I completely understand.

She starts talking about friends again but I stop her.

I already made one, I tell her. *In fact I have seven little dwarf friends.*

She tilts her head. Then she shakes it. *I'm talking about real people Caitlin.*

Me too. They're first graders. I think. At least Michael is.

She does her turtle neck jerk. *Michael Schneider?*

I don't know. Does he wear a red Potomac Nationals baseball cap?

He often does. Caitlin. Do you remember the name of the teacher who was killed at the middle school?

Of course. It was Mrs. Roberta L. Schneider. And then I think about Michael's last name. *Oh. Are they related?*

Mrs. Brook nods. *Michael's mother.*

I knew his mother was dead but I didn't know she was shot like Devon. *Is that why he was at the memorial service?*

Yes. I think all of us were at the memorial service. We're a small enough town that we're like one big family. But . . . still . . . how odd for you two to find each other.

It's not odd, I say. *I'm at little kid recess now. Remember? And he was crying the first time I saw him so I was being nice to him. And he knew about Devon. He said I was the weirdo whose—*

The what? Mrs. Brook jerks her neck again.

He didn't really mean weirdo. He said he was sorry. He's nice. And so am I. So it's not odd *for us to be friends.*

She smiles. *You're right. I think you and Michael have a very important friendship.*

Me too. I'm glad I have stickers and gummy worms for him.

When little kid recess starts I give Michael more planet stickers and all the gummy worms in my pocket.

Thanks! He looks at the worms. *What are their names?*

I start to name them but then I stop. *You can name them.*

He grins. He dangles the orange one in front of me and then the red. *This is Henry and this is Mudge.*

Like in the book, I say.

He nods. *And these two green ones are Frog and Toad. Have you read those books?*

I have all of those books.

Me too, he says. *Hey guess what!*

What?

My teacher says we're getting fifth-grade reading buddies! Will you be my buddy?

I haven't heard anything about fifth-grade buddies. I don't know if I'm doing it. Maybe they do it during first recess when I have Mrs. Brook time.

He shakes his head. *Nope. It's at the end of the day. It starts Thursday.*

Oh. I wonder if Mrs. Johnson told us and I just wasn't listening. Sometimes that happens. A lot.

Hey guess what? Michael says. *It's Tyler's birthday. We got cookies with gummy bears on them.*

Lucky.

And he's having a skating party on Saturday. What kind of party are you having?

What?

You said your birthday is next month.

It is.

So what kind of party are you having?

I don't have parties.

Oh. What do you do?

I go to the mall with my brother.

His Bambi eyes open wide and he doesn't say anything for a few seconds. *Isn't your brother dead?*

Yes. But I still want to do it.

He nods slowly. *I know. I still want to do stuff with my mom too.*

I feel glowy and warm because Michael Gets It. *My dad doesn't Get It,* I tell him.

My dad doesn't Get It either.

Does he still want to play football?

Michael sighs. *All the time.*

He must really love football.

Yeah. I don't think he's very good at it though.

Why not?

I heard my grandmother say that he's keeping his head up but pretty soon he's going to crash and burn.

I turn and Look At The Person. *You mean in a car accident?*

Michael Looks At The Person too. *No. It means he's going to be really bad at something. My grandmother says that kind of stuff all the time. She says shake a leg when she wants you to hurry and perk up your ears when she wants you to listen and be a doll when she wants you to get her a glass of iced tea.*

I can't help giggling. I try to picture a doll holding a glass of iced tea.

Michael laughs too. *Want to know my favorite thing she*

says? When she wants you to be patient she says . . . keep your pants on!

I laugh too. *Why would you take your pants off?*

I don't know! He howls.

And we both end up giggling until the bell rings.

When I get home I remember what Mrs. Brook said about Dad and Devon and I have a plan to make everything okay. I sit on the sofa and start talking about Devon a lot except I don't call him Devon anymore. I call him Devon-who-is-dead. I say it until Dad asks me to stop.

But that's his name.

No. His name is Devon.

No. His name WAS Devon. Now it's Devon-who-is-dead. That's different from the other Devon. That Devon was alive and you thought I was confused but I'm not because I know that Devon is dead and that's why I'm calling him Devon-who-is-dead and you'll get used to it.

No I won't. I'll feel like crying every time you say it.

Even if I say it fifty times?

Yes.

Even a hundred times?

Yes.

Even a thousand times?

Caitlin. I get upset even thinking about it so I'll definitely feel like crying every time you say it.

I'm only saying it because you're upset that I think Devon is still alive so I'm showing you I Get It that Devon is dead.

Dad shakes his head and leaves the living room.

I stare at the chest and wish for the millionth time that Devon were here because even when I try to Get It I still don't Get It.

CHAPTER **18**

A PLAN
FOR HEALING

MICHAEL IS RIGHT. WE ARE DOING
reading buddies. When my class walks into the
library Michael's class is already sitting in a
circle on the floor crisscross-applesauce. We
open and close our hands three times to each
other. It's our special wave. He's grinning so
much it reminds me to smile.

Mrs. Brook is there too and she's also smiling. *Hi Caitlin.*

I start shaking my hands. *It's not Mrs. Brook time yet. I have to read to Michael.*

Her smile goes away too. *Actually we're pairing Michael and Josh up.*

I Look At The Person. *Why? He's evil!*

Josh stands up and stares at me. He blinks fast and sits down again.

Shhh! Caitlin! Mrs. Brook whispers. *That's not nice.*

I wasn't talking about Michael, I tell her.

I realize that. She is still whispering.

You are making a mistake.

We're . . . She smiles. *We're working on Closure here.*

I look around the room. *Where is it? Because that's what I'm working on and I'd like to see it.*

She takes me out into the hall and explains that Josh is going through a lot right now too just like Michael and me. And that Josh needs to see that not everyone's mad at him and Michael needs to see that Josh can be a very nice boy. *I call it a Plan for Healing,* she says.

I Look At The Person. *A Plan for Healing is a stupid plan because Josh cannot be a very nice boy. Haven't you seen him push people off the monkey bars? Do you know what he says to people?*

I do. And none of that is okay. But he has been getting counseling too and we're working through his hurt so he can get to Closure.

What about ME? I'M the one who wants Closure!

Part of your Plan for Healing is to make friends. Right?

I AM making friends and now you're giving him to Josh!

You can both be friends with the same person.

She doesn't Get It. *Michael is MY friend. I want to be the one who reads to him!*

You can read to him during recess or other times but for our once-a-week reading buddies it's going to be Josh and Michael.

The rest of the stupid reading buddies time is a blur. I know I read really LOUD so Michael can hear me reading to HIM even though I am at the other end of the library. I know that the stupid little girl I'm reading to starts crying because she says I'm yelling at her which I'm not. If the book says STOP! then that's how you should read it. Especially if Michael is sitting next to Josh and especially if Josh is giving Michael a high five and ESPECIALLY if Michael and Josh are giggling together. And I know Mrs. Brook takes me out of the library early but not before I see Michael looking at me with his big Bambi eyes and giving me our special wave.

At home I go to my hidey-hole in Devon's room. I take his piece of notebook paper with me. The one that says *EAGLE SCOUT PROJECT.* The one with the list of supplies for his chest. The one that says he's going to teach me. I stare at the list trying to find Closure. I keep hoping that somehow the Devon-ness of the list will give me the answer but it doesn't.

I look up at Devon's carving of SCOUT and wonder if I can still be Scout if the person who called me Scout is now gone. I still want to be Scout for him. Devon said, *If you want to be a Scout you have to Work At It.* I know he was talking about Boy Scouts and Eagle Scouts but he also said that about anything I had to do. *You have to Work At It Scout. I KNOW,* I told him because he said it a lot lot lot and sometimes I don't want to hear the same thing over and over and over. Especially if it's hard. And Work At It is VERY hard. I Work At It ALL the time. My whole day is Work At It. Sometimes I don't want to Work At It anymore. Like when

I FINALLY get my own friend and then Mrs. Brook TAKES HIM AWAY FROM ME! It's just—too—HARD! It's—NOT—FAIR!

I hear Dad calling my name but I don't want to come out of my hidey-hole. I'm busy stuffed-animaling the carving of SCOUT. It's warm and soft and quiet and safe in here. And I don't have to Work At It. I'm thinking about staying here. Living here. Forever.

Finally when Dad says, *Answer me please Caitlin!* I answer because he asked nicely.

The door opens. *Caitlin?* His voice sounds funny. *Are you in here?*

I'm under the dresser.

What are you doing in here?

Thinking.

Thinking about what?

Thinking I'm going to stay here and make this my room now.

Oh? Why?

It was always supposed to be mine. I asked Devon if I could have it.

He's quiet for a minute. Then he takes a deep breath. *When Devon was gone to college.*

He IS gone.

I hear the squishy breathy sound of Devon's mattress squishing. *But . . . he's not just gone to college. He's gone . . . forever.*

I don't tell Dad that I didn't ask Devon if I could have his room when he was gone. I asked him a different way.

And Devon said it was a weird way and I shouldn't say it like that and I asked why.

He said people would get upset.

I don't want Dad to get upset.

So I don't say what I really said: *Can I have your room when you're dead?*

I think maybe I understand what Devon meant. Because now I have a recess feeling in my stomach.

I slide out from my hidey-hole and crawl past Dad's shoes to my room. I get a clean piece of paper and make a sign. It says, *Devon's Room,* and I draw Devon's eyes in the top left corner. In the top right corner I draw his mouth with his lips curled up to show he's happy. I draw his crooked nose in the bottom left corner. His chest is in the bottom right corner. It's still not finished. And I guess it never will be.

CHAPTER **19**

SHOES

EARLY TUESDAY MORNING RA-
chel Lockwood comes into class and her face is
scratched up and purple. Her left arm and leg
are bandaged. Everyone crowds around her
saying, *Oh my gosh! What happened? Are you
okay?*

I fell off my bike, Rachel says.

How? someone asks.

*I was riding past the middle school and I heard
sirens and I thought there was another shooting.*

Oh my gosh! Was there? a girl asks.

No—duh! a boy says. *We would've heard by now.*

Rachel shakes her head. *No. But I was watching the police car coming up the road so I wasn't watching where I was going and I went off the sidewalk and fell off my bike.* She looks down. *It really hurt. I was riding so fast to try to get away because I was scared of being shot like . . .* She stops talking and turns to me. So does everyone else. It is very quiet.

You should watch where you're going when you're riding a bike, I tell her. That's what Devon always told me.

Some people turn away and some shake their heads but I know I'm right. Emma and some of the other girls stand around Rachel so she is in the middle of a circle and they are all staring at her. I wouldn't like that so I stare at them and hope they get the message to leave her alone.

Finally Rachel asks if her face looks really bad and Emma says, *Of course not. It looks totally fine.*

Rachel says, *Really?* She looks around and her eyes stop at me.

I look away because I wasn't staring at her like those other girls.

What? she asks. Her voice is soft and shaky. *Does my face look bad?*

Even though I'm not looking at her I can feel her Look At The Person. I wonder how she knows that honesty is one of my skills. *Yes,* I say. *It looks bad. It's purple and puffy and really gross.*

Rachel starts crying and runs out of the room.

CAITLIN! Emma yells. *That was so mean! Didn't anyone ever tell you how to be a friend?*

That's when I realize that maybe I should listen to Mrs. Brook when she talks about friends. Now that Devon isn't here to tell me.

I try to say that purple is actually my favorite color but too many of the girls are yelling at me. They say that Rachel will be self-conscious and embarrassed and it's all my fault.

I hate self-conscious and embarrassed. I decide to help Rachel. I'm a very helpful person. I look around the room but I know there's no place for her to hide. There's no sofa or blanket or anyplace where she can be in her Personal Space and not have people staring at her.

Then I have an idea. I pull her desk out of the row and push it all the way to the back corner of the room and shove it up against the wall where the terrarium was until the turtle died.

I hear voices saying, *What is she doing?*

She's such a weirdo!

She's finally cracked!

But I don't care. I'm being a friend.

I go back and get Rachel's chair and put it under her desk so it's facing the corner. Now no one can see her face and she can hide from everyone. I'm happy until Emma and Rachel come back and Rachel starts crying again and Emma starts yelling and pulls the desk out of the corner and I try to stop her and Mrs. Johnson comes in and says, *What in the world is going on?*

Emma says how mean I'm being and Mrs. Johnson gives me her pinched lip stern look and says, *What's this all about?* And I tell her I'm just trying to be a friend.

Some of the boys laugh but the girls are mad and Mrs.

Johnson takes me all the way to Mrs. Brook's room herself even though I know how to get there.

I sit at Mrs. Brook's table and cry because even though I Work At It I still don't Get It. *I was being a friend!*

I know you were, Mrs. Brook says, *and I know that you might feel comforted by sitting in the corner and not having people look at you but Rachel doesn't.*

Why not?

To Rachel it felt like you didn't want to see her so you wanted to get rid of her by putting her in a corner.

That's not what I meant!

I know but try to put yourself in her shoes.

I Look At The Person.

Empathy, Mrs. Brook says. *Remember? It means to try to feel the way someone else is feeling. You step out of your own shoes and put on someone else's because you're trying to BE that person for a moment. In Rachel's case you want to try to feel how she might feel having all those obvious injuries.*

I can't because it didn't happen to ME. I don't have ban-

dages or a purple scratched-up face so how am I supposed to know how it feels?

I think you can learn empathy. Mrs. Brook smiles at me. *In fact I'm sure of it.* She goes on to explain life the way Rachel sees it.

I listen but I don't want to tell her that it's not life how I see it. I also don't want to tell her that I'm not sure I can learn how to do empathy. She seems so sure that I can.

I look down at my shoes. Quietly I slip them off. My feet feel cold and clammy because my socks are sweaty. I carefully touch my toes onto the floor which is hard and cold. I pull my feet off of the floor and shove them back into my sneakers. At least I tried dipping my toe in empathy.

CHAPTER **20**

EMPATHY

I STARE AT THE SIGN I PUT ON Devon's door for a long time. I realize they are the first eyes I have ever drawn. And how much they look like Devon's. I wonder how the picture would look if I put the eyes together with the broken nose and his mouth. It would be a complete face. Of Devon. And I would always know what he looked like even when I grow up. He could always be with me.

I wonder if putting a whole face together

would help bring me closer to Closure. If it's split apart into pieces then wouldn't putting all the pieces together bring Closure? But I've never done a whole face before. I don't want to mess it up. It has to be right.

I hear Dad turning off Fox Five News and sighing. I remember what Mrs. Brook said about practicing empathy and I go into the living room and look at Dad's shoes.

Hi Dad.

Hi Caitlin.

I'm not sure what to say next. His shoes don't give me any clues. *Um . . . so how are you?*

Dad looks up from the sofa. *Actually I'm dealing with a lot of stuff right now.*

Oh. Are you looking for Closure?

In a way. Yes.

Me too. Maybe you can come see Mrs. Brook. She said you could do that sometimes even though mostly she has to see the kids at school.

Dad nods.

Maybe you could see someone else too.

Dad doesn't say anything. He doesn't even nod.

Maybe you could find some answers in books.

Thanks Caitlin. I appreciate it but I'll figure out a way.

When?

I don't know. I think it'll take a long long time.

How are you going to do it?

I don't even know where to begin. He stares at the rug. Even when the phone rings.

Phone, I tell him.

It rings again. *Phone.*

And again. *PHONE,* I say LOUD in case he didn't hear.

Please answer it, he says.

I get a recess feeling in my stomach. I hate answering the phone. I don't know who it will be or what they will say.

The phone rings two more times.

CAITLIN PLEASE!

I run to the phone and grab it because I hate shouting even worse than the phone. At least you can hang up the phone.

Hello, says the voice. *Hello?*

It sounds like Aunt Jolee.

Is anyone there?

Dad and I are here, I say.

Oh Caitlin! It's you. Hi!

I wait for her to talk more.

Are you still there?

Yes.

Oh. I wasn't sure because you weren't talking.

That's because you were talking and it's rude to talk when someone else is talking.

Oh . . . well . . . so . . . what are you up to?

Talking on the phone. With you.

Can I speak with your dad?

I look at the sofa. Dad is still staring at the spot on the rug. *He's dealing with a lot of stuff right now. But he won't read any books about it or go see Mrs. Brook or any other counselor.*

Dad looks up from the sofa. *Who is it?*

Aunt Jolee. I think. Wait. Is this Aunt Jolee?

Yup! You guessed!

It's Aunt Jolee.

He oofs like all the air goes out of him when he stands up and reaches for the phone.

I give it to him.

He leans against the wall. *Hi Jo-Jo.*

Jo-Jo is Dad's name for Aunt Jolee. It's a nickname. Like

Scout. Dad is Aunt Jolee's big brother. Like Jem. Like Devon. Like Devon WAS. Dad still has Aunt Jolee's finger-painted handprint from when she was in kindergarten. It's in a little blue frame on the wall by the TV. It says TO HARE on it because when she was five she wasn't very smart and couldn't spell Dad's name the right way which is Harry.

Dad shakes his head while he talks to Aunt Jolee. *I can't afford to see a counselor.*

Silence.

What insurance? I don't have any insurance.

Silence.

Do you know how much it costs to see a counselor?

Silence.

Even clinics charge something unless you make no money at all and I'm not quitting my job just so I can see a counselor.

Silence.

Yes I'm sure it'd help her but she's got the counselor at school at least. I don't know what else to do.

Silence.

I know Jo-Jo. Of course you can't leave them. They're too young. Dad is nodding. *I wish you lived closer too. You're still my best . . . friend.* When he says the word friend a cry comes out of him.

He slides down the wall and sits on the floor. He drops his head and tries to cover it with the hand that's not holding the phone but I can see his head shaking along with his hand and the phone. I can hear him sniffing too. Then he takes a deep breath and looks up at Aunt Jolee's handprint on the wall and says, *Thank you.*

I try not to listen to Dad because I've had all the empathy I can take right now. Empathy can make you feel really sad.

I put my head under the sofa cushion and peek out at Devon's chest.

I hear Dad say *Thank you* again.

I keep staring at Devon's chest because it makes me feel like a little bit of him is still here. Even though I know he'll never be able to teach me how to make a chest. Even though he won't be able to teach me anything. Even though I'll never see him again and won't ever be able to look at him and say, *Thank you.*

The more I look at the chest the more I start turning it from a sharp-shaped sheet into something soft. I guess I'm stuffed-animaling even though I don't mean to. It's easy when your eyes are already blurry.

CHAPTER **21**

NO MRS. BROOK

THE REST OF THE CLASS RUNS out of the classroom to go to recess. I get up to go to Mrs. Brook time and I decide to ask her if Dad can come see her since she doesn't charge insurance. At least she never charges me insurance. And she said she could see him even though he's a grown-up.

Mrs. Johnson says, *Oh Caitlin. I almost forgot. Mrs. Brook isn't here.*

I know. She's in her room.

No. She had to go out of town.

Why?

Her sister is having difficulty with her pregnancy.

I Look At The Person.

Mrs. Johnson looks at the floor and then at me. *She's having a lot of trouble with her twin babies who aren't born yet.*

I thought babies were only a lot of trouble after they were born.

Sometimes it's before and after. So Mrs. Brook is going to see what she can do to help her sister. She sighs. *I hope everything goes well.*

I wonder what that means. *What if it doesn't?*

I just mean I hope the babies . . . are fine.

What if they're not? What'll be wrong with them?

I'm sure they'll be fine. Pregnancy is just . . . hard.

How does she know? *Are you pregnant?*

Mrs. Johnson's face turns pinkish. *N-no.*

I don't want to be pregnant either, I say. *I have enough hard things to Deal With.*

Mrs. Johnson lets me sit in the classroom instead of going to recess. She gives me paper so I can draw. I decide to draw a picture for Mrs. Brook of some stuffed animals looking at the Facial Expressions Chart because I have that chart memorized.

Mrs. Johnson says I should write a letter to Mrs. Brook to go with my drawing. I sigh because I'd rather draw but Mrs. Johnson Looks At The Person hard so I write the letter even though I'm much better at drawing than writing and Mrs. Johnson should know that by now.

Dear Mrs. Brook I'm sorry about your difficult sister and the babies who are still inside of her causing trouble. I hope they start behaving so you can come back soon. I will even practice my finesse and keep pace with you when we walk. And I promise I will be your friend. Scout's honor.

Caitlin Ann Smith.

CHAPTER 22

DRAWINGS

DAD SAYS WE'RE GOING TO A FUN
raiser for the families of the people who were
shot. He says it's being given by people who
care about us and want to help us and even
though I don't like crowds we still have to go
because we have to show we appreciate what
they're doing for us and we should act like we
appreciate it and like we want to be there even

if we don't because no one has to do a fun raiser but they're doing it anyway.

I want to go, I tell him, *so you can stop making excuses.* A fun raiser sounds like a good thing.

He stops talking. He tilts his head like he doesn't Get It. I don't know why.

What kind of fun things will there be? I ask.

He shrugs. *I think there's a silent auction and a raffle and I'm not sure what else.*

Oh. That doesn't sound like much fun.

Cait-LIN, he says in his warning voice.

Okay okay.

The fun raiser is in the Virginia Dare Middle School cafeteria. When we get out of the car near the cafeteria door Dad stops and stares at the school for a moment. He blinks a lot and swallows hard so the lump that sticks out of his throat keeps going in and out. Finally he takes a sharp breath before he pulls the door open.

The noise spills out and it smells like soggy spaghetti and the light makes me squint. Almost immediately bodies cover us like we are germs and they are the white blood cells sent to surround and destroy us. I think I will choke. I grab Dad's hand. It's big and hairy and sweaty but I Deal With It because otherwise I think I will be smothered.

This is my daughter Caitlin, Dad says.

Hello Caitlin, a voice says. *How are you?*

I keep looking at the ground. Dad's head comes down to my face. *Remember to Look At The Person and say something nice.*

I don't Look At The Person but I say nice stuff. *I'm ten. My birthday is next month. My favorite color is purple. My favorite game is Mario Kart but any video game is fine. My favorite video is* Bambi *except lately I don't like it so much.*

Oh . . . well . . . that's nice, the voice says, and the body moves away.

Dad says, *Not so much about yourself next time.*

I try to tell him I'm being helpful because I'm giving people information about what I want for my birthday in case they want to buy me something but Dad introduces me to another person.

This time I Look At The Hat which at least is close to The Person. The Hat is the size of an umbrella and that gives me an idea of what to say. *When people say it's raining cats and dogs it isn't really. That just means it's raining a lot. But it can rain frogs if they get sucked up in a storm and they plop down on top of your head. Also snow can be pink if red dirt dissolves in water that evaporates and—*

Dad squeezes my shoulder. This means the conversation is over.

Another voice shouts *Hi Caitlin!* and a big hand comes into my Personal Space so I back up.

Say hello, Dad says.

Hello.

Look At The Person, Dad reminds me.

I keep my head down but tilt it enough to see one of his ears.

Dad says, *Cait-LIN,* in his warning voice.

What? That's closer than The Hat!

Say something nice, Dad hisses.

When Dad hisses he is serious. He will not let me leave until I say something nice. I try to focus. I stare at the ear. What can I say that's nice? Finally I realize and say it. *I don't think you're disgusting just because you have hair sticking out of your ear.*

Dad pulls me away by both shoulders which means the conversation is over NOW.

I look around for Michael because his mother was shot like Devon so he should be at the fun raiser too. I know he's Josh's friend now and not mine but I don't like all of these people so I wish I could at least see him. Suddenly a face is in front of mine and coffee breath goes up my nostrils and a voice says, *I have someone I bet you'd like to meet.*

I bet she's wrong.

She grabs the hand that isn't holding Dad and I yank it away from her.

I'll go with you, Dad says.

We follow Coffee Breath Woman to an easel with a light on it and I stare at it.

See? I thought you'd like Mr. Walters.

I don't know who or where Mr. Walters is but I do like the easel. There is a cartoon picture of a boy on it. He has a tiny body and a huge head. His mouth is grinning so much that his cheeks push his eyes up at the corners so even his eyes look happy like the photos of eyes that Mrs. Brook has shown me about a million times.

A man's hand appears and adds tufts of sticky-outy hair to the giant head.

I laugh. Maybe this will be a fun raiser after all.

You like it? a man's voice says.

I nod. Normally I don't talk to strangers but if he can draw like this he can't be that strange.

I'm Charlie Walters the middle school art teacher, the voice says. *Shall I do your picture?*

I do my own pictures, I tell him.

I mean, shall I draw a picture of you?

No. Why would I want a picture of me?

Your dad here might want a picture of you.

I shake my head. *He sees me every day. He doesn't need a picture.*

But this is a different kind of picture. This captures personality and emotion.

I Look At The Person. I look at the hand with his pencil. It's just a charcoal pencil. Like mine.

He chuckles. *You don't believe me?*

I shake my head.

I'll show you. Sit down over there.

No. I want to watch you capturing someone's emotion.

Draw me, Dad says, and he sits on a little stool beyond the easel.

I watch the cartoon character grow from a potato head to

a porcupine head to a Dad head. Mr. Walters puts the ears on the head first then a nose then a mouth. He squints at Dad for a while before he even draws the eyes. He is very careful with the eyes. He draws them in stages from the outside in. He doesn't stop when he gets to the inside though. He takes a blue pencil and draws little colored dots and lines that make the eyes look deep and textured and full. And something else too. They look sad. I stare at Dad's real eyes and I think I see the sad there too although it's easier for me to see it in the picture. The picture doesn't blink or look away.

You should do the Facial Expressions Chart at school, I tell Mr. Walters. *You would do a much better job than the one we have now.*

He nods once and smiles. *Thank you very much.* He pulls the sheet of paper off the easel and gives it to Dad and hands me a charcoal pencil. *Would you like to try drawing me now?*

I'm not so good with people. Or emotions.

I think you're observant though and that's the first step.

I Look At The Person. I stare into his eyes. His eyes look happy but not a mean laughy kind of happy. *Are you happy?*

Yes. Now let's see if you can draw that.

He is still holding his charcoal pencil out to me so I take it.

Mr. Walters gets up and walks over to the stool and sits down facing me.

Dad is standing behind me. *Go ahead. Draw Mr. Walters.*

Well don't WATCH me! I can't draw if you're going to watch.

All right. I'll wander around the room and look at other things. Okay?

Okay. If there's a fishing booth let me know because those always have good prizes. And if there are any gummy worms grab some before they're all gone. Please.

I stare at the huge blank paper in front of me. Usually I only have small pieces of paper.

I see a hand waving around the outside of the easel. *Yoo-hoo! You have to look over here.*

I peek around the easel. It's Mr. Walters.

Start with the outside of my head like I did with your dad.

So I do. I make a Mr. Potato Head. Then I add hair but only a little because Mr. Walters doesn't have much. The nose is easy and so are the ears. The mouth is harder because usually I look at mouths when there are words coming out and right now there are none coming out of his. It's flat. I do notice some curves and creases though so I put them in.

Feel free to use the colored pencils or pastels too, he says.

I shake my head. *I don't use colors. My drawings are black and white with no blurry stuff. It's easier to see that way.* Blurry is good for stuffed-animaling but not for drawing.

Mr. Walters tilts his head like he doesn't Get It but I don't want to explain right now because I'm busy drawing.

Wow, a voice behind me says. *That's so awesome! Did you really draw that?*

I put my arms over the picture to cover it up before turning around to see Emma from school.

Let's see it, she says.

No.

Come on! Keep going! I want to watch!

I can't do it if you're watching, I tell her.

Please?

No!

A hand squeezes Emma's shoulder. A woman's voice says, *Let's give her some space and we can come back when she's done.*

Emma makes a snorty sound but moves away.

Good. I'm still stuck on the eyes of my picture however and I stare at the paper.

You need to look at my eyes, Mr. Walters says.

I sigh. *Are you related to Mrs. Brook?*

No. Why?

She always wants me to look in her eyes too.

Eyes are the windows to the soul, Mr. Walters says. *If you look inside the eyes you can see so much about a person.*

I Look At The Person including his eyes. *Really?*

He smiles and nods.

But there is something wrong with his smile. I stare into his eyes. Maybe what's wrong is his eyes. They don't look happy like the photos of happy eyes Mrs. Brook has shown me. Maybe his smile is not big enough to push his eyes up at the corners like happy eyes are supposed to be. *Something's wrong,* I tell him.

Why do you say that?

Your eyes and mouth don't match.

Ah, he says as he nods. *Maybe you're better at emotions than you think.*

Except I don't know which is right.

141

Both. I'm smiling because I think you're a wonderful talented girl. My eyes are sad because I'm thinking about what you and your dad are going through.

I think for a minute about what he means. *Oh. Because of Devon.*

Yes. Because of Devon. He was in my class one quarter. I miss him. Everyone here misses him.

Why do you miss him? You're the art teacher. He can't even draw.

We all have different passions. His passion was being an Eagle Scout.

He won't be able to finish his chest though so he can't ever make Eagle.

He nods. *I heard about that chest.* His voice is crackly. *It's so hard.*

Devon says if it's hard that just means you have to Work At It.

He shrugs but sniffs too much to talk.

Maybe you need to find Closure.

He Looks At The Person. *I think we all need to find Closure. It hurt the whole community. We're all sad.* His eyes are so sad now they are starting to water.

I put the pencil down on the easel tray. *I don't feel like drawing anymore.*

He jumps up from the stool. *I'm sorry. I didn't mean to make you feel sad.* He looks at the paper on the easel. *Wow. That is amazing. Don't you want to give the eyes a try?*

I shake my head. *I don't think I can do a complete face yet.* Maybe later.

He pulls his eyeless picture off the easel and hands it to me.

After Dad is in bed I sneak into Devon's room and tape Mr. Walters on the wall next to my picture of the eagle. This is the first picture of a face I've ever done. Even if it doesn't have eyes.

CHAPTER 23

LOST

ON TUESDAY NIGHT I WALK INTO
the kitchen and Dad is standing at the sink.

What's for dinner? I ask.

He turns around fast and his eyes are big
which means surprise I think. Except why
would he be surprised when he knows I live
here?

What? I say.

I'm sorry. He turns back to the sink. *I was
lost . . .*

You're in the kitchen, I tell him. *It's next to the living room. Then there's the hall that goes to—*

I know Caitlin. What I meant was I'm feeling a little lost. He grips the edge of the sink. *You'll be starting at the . . . middle school . . . next year.*

No. I'll be starting at the middle school in August. That's this year.

He turns and Looks At The Person. *Are you—* He stops and puts his hand over his mouth. Then he takes it away again. *Are you okay with going to . . . that school?*

Virginia Dare?

He sucks in his breath when I say it.

Devon's school?

He closes his eyes.

I shrug. *I guess. They don't have recess in middle school and I don't like recess.*

Dad opens his eyes but he still stares at the air. *If I could afford to pay for a private school for you I would.*

People talk about private schools but I don't know exactly what they are. So I ask. *Does private mean I'm the only one in the school? Because I'd like that a lot.*

No. Of course not.

145

So it's just like a regular school?

Pretty much.

I shake my head. *Then I don't want private. I'm fine with the regular one.*

He nods and lets out a big breath. *Okay.*

CHAPTER **24**

FOUND

I DON'T HAVE MY MRS. BROOK
time because she's still visiting her difficult
sister.

Instead I have to go to recess with the rest
of the class and miss little kid recess. I lost my
friend in little kid recess anyway so I don't really mind. What I do mind is passing Michael's
class in the hall on the way back and seeing
Josh give him a high five. I don't look at Michael but he says, *HI CAITLIN!* even though

there is No Talking In The Halls and out of the edge of my eye I see him give me our special wave except I don't think it's so special anymore so I don't wave back.

My class goes to the computer lab. Mrs. Johnson says we have free time and can look up any topic we want to learn more about as long as it's not computer games. I read about Eagle Scouts and Eagle Scout projects. None of them are as good as Devon's chest. Except that they're finished.

I get a recess feeling in my stomach and try not to think about the Eagle Scout project that never got to exist. Or the Eagle Scout. I start stuffed-animaling the computer monitor with the window behind it into one big grayish blur until I hear Mrs. Johnson's voice in my ear that we have three minutes left and if there's one last thing we want to look up now is the time.

I suddenly remember I should be researching Closure because maybe there's even a better definition than in my Dictionary so I look it up and this is what I find:

—the act of bringing to an end; a conclusion
—example: *They finally brought the project to closure.*

I see Devon's Eagle Scout project in my head and think about how much he wanted to finish it and become an Eagle Scout. And how he was going to teach me how to do woodworking too. And then I start shaking my hands fast and my Heart is pounding in my ears and it's hard to breathe and I hear moaning and it must be me because Mrs. Johnson says, *Caitlin are you all right?* And I hear myself scream to the whole world and I think in my head, *Now I know how to experience an emotional conclusion to a difficult life event!* and Mrs. Johnson is gripping my shoulders and shaking me and I don't even mind and she screams, *What is it? What is it?* and I shout loud enough for Devon to hear me up in Heaven, *I GET IT! I GET IT! I GET IT! I GET IT!*

C H A P T E R **25**

HINGES

WHEN DAD PICKS ME UP EARLY
at school he starts asking me about my TRM
but I tell him, *We need to go to Lowe's!*

What?

Right now!

What's all this about, Caitlin?

Closure! Drive fast!

His voice keeps going but I'm too busy
bouncing in the backseat to hear the words.

I run into Lowe's and race up and down

the aisles and Dad is chasing me saying, *Caitlin Caitlin!*
Excuse me ma'am! Sorry! Caitlin! Excuse me! until I find the
place with the hinges and I'm panting with excitement and
I shake my hands for Dad to hurry up and he's panting too
and says, *CAIT-LIN!* but I say, *Which ones?* as I rattle the
different-sized boxes of hinges.

He is still panting but doesn't say anything right away
until he says, *What are you talking about?*

THE HINGES! Which ones do we need?

He tilts his head. *For what?*

THE CHEST! Why doesn't he Get It?

Chest?

DEVON'S CHEST! HIS EAGLE SCOUT PROJECT!

Dad's shoulders slump and his head falls. He puts a
hand on his forehead and closes his eyes.

Can I help you? a man in a red apron says.

I look at Dad. He is not helping so I say, *Yes,* even though
I don't like talking to strangers. *We need hinges for the chest.*

What kind of hinges?

I Look At The Person. *You are no help either.*

He looks at Dad.

We don't need any hinges today, Dad says quietly.

Why not? I ask.

I'm not ready to work on the chest.

I am.

We need to talk about this first.

Okay. Talk.

At home.

Then we'll have to come right back to Lowe's again.

Later, he says.

What time?

I don't know.

Can't we just talk about this in the car and then come back in again?

He turns and starts walking down the aisle passing people who look at him and then at me. When he gets to the end of the aisle and turns right and disappears I am left with all the strangers staring at me. I start crying and run down the aisle screaming for Dad and even though I find him I cry all the way to the car and all the way home and for a long time in my hidey-hole in Devon's room wrapped up in my purple fleece because Dad says he is not interested in working on the chest and not to ask him again for a very long time.

CHAPTER **26**

EAGLE SCOUT

I GET A SPECIAL PHONE CALL AT school. It's from Mrs. Brook. I get to go all the way to the office and talk on the phone at the front desk. Mrs. Brook says she just wants to talk to me personally and see how I'm doing because she can't come back to school for a few more days.

I tell her all about how I finally found Closure but Dad won't cooperate even though I know how to get us there.

She says I have to be patient and keep trying. *Sometimes things don't work the first time but then eventually they do.*

Like finesse?

Exactly.

And making friends?

Yes.

Even for me?

Absolutely. I have confidence in you. You just have to keep trying.

Josh is walking into the principal's office when I get off the phone.

He turns his head to me and whispers, *Loser.*

I know, I tell him, *but I'm going to keep trying.*

He shakes his head and snorts.

I guess he doesn't believe I will Get It and sometimes I'm not so sure either but Mrs. Brook is confident so I'm going to keep working on my finesse.

Later that day I see Michael in the hall. I won't see him at recess because while Mrs. Brook is away my schedule is back to first recess only. Even though he is not my friend anymore I do say, *I found Closure but I still have to Work At It.*

I had to tell him. I promised. Scout's honor.

He looks at me funny so I decide he doesn't want to be my friend anyway.

I find a white T-shirt in my closet and I draw an eagle on it with a permanent marker. I'm hoping that Dad will remember that Devon called me Scout and he'll put the two together like this:

EAGLE + SCOUT

and he will think of Devon's Eagle Scout project and we can work on it together.

Except he doesn't notice.

I keep walking back and forth in front of the sofa.

Finally he says, *Do you have to go to the bathroom?*

No, I say. *Do you like my T-shirt?*

Mmm-hmmm.

I sigh. *It's EAGLE SCOUT. Get It?*

Dad tilts his head.

It's a picture of an eagle and I'm Scout.

Oh.

So are you ready to work on the chest yet?

He shakes his head.

Dad. We need to finish the chest.

He shakes his head again.

Why not?

We don't even have all the wood.

We can buy some.

It's special wood.

How special?

It's a Mission chest.

What does that mean?

It's a style of furniture that requires quarter-cut oak. The wood is expensive and it's difficult to work with.

But I can help. It can be a group project. Mrs. Brook says I need to practice working on group projects so this will be perfect.

Dad leaves the living room.

I think about quarter-cut oak and how I still don't actually know what that means. I know what an oak is. We have an oak tree in the backyard. I know what a quarter is. I have forty-seven in my State Quarters Map because Illinois and Florida and Iowa fell out and are under my bed somewhere

I think. And I know what it means to cut something. I look up quarter-cut in my Dictionary but there's no definition. I guess I have to put it together myself so quarter-cut oak is oak you cut with a quarter.

I have forty-six quarters in my State Quarters Map now because Virginia is coming out to cut the oak tree.

CHAPTER **27**

MISSION

ALL I CAN SAY IS IT WILL TAKE my whole entire life to get some wood cut out of that oak tree with my Virginia quarter. Monday is a teacher workday so between Sunday and Monday I have spent six hours and thirteen minutes cutting that stupid tree. I will never get a whole piece of wood out of there. Plus my fingers are all bloody from scraping the bumpy bark and they hurt.

. . .

Mrs. Brook is back from visiting her difficult sister and the babies who are finally born now. It has been so long since I've seen her that when I get to her room I hold my hand up and wave to say hi.

She screams. This is not the reaction I expect. She should say something like, *I missed you,* or, *It's good to see you again*. That's what teachers normally say.

Caitlin, Mrs. Brook says, *why are there cuts on your fingers?* Her voice is high and shaky. *What have you been doing?*

Cutting.

What? It comes out as a scream. Her hand covers her mouth. *Why?* That comes out as a muffled crying moan.

I need the wood.

Her hand drops and she tilts her head. *Excuse me?*

For Closure.

Can you explain from the beginning?

Yes. I can but it's a long story so I'd rather not.

I mean would you please start explaining now. Her voice is getting shaky again.

Okay. Fine. Dad doesn't want to work on the chest and

whenever I ask him if we can work on it because I'm trying to get to Closure he says we can't because we need more wood but it has to be quarter-cut oak and Dad says that's too hard to get but we have an oak tree and I have a quarter so I've been trying to get a piece of wood cut out of it.

Oh, Caitlin! You poor thing! She covers her mouth again. *And you've been working so hard!*

Yes. Dad's right about how hard it is. Now I Get It.

Well, she says, *I don't know exactly what quarter-cut oak is but I do know this much: it is not wood cut from an oak tree with a quarter.*

Oh. I guess I don't Get It then.

I'm going to call your father.

Why?

I want to ask him what quarter-cut oak is and tell him how hard you've been working to get it.

Here's the funny thing. Quarter-cut oak just means the way the oak tree is cut into boards for Mission furniture like Devon's Mission chest. I wish Dad would just tell me these things. It would make life a lot easier.

CHAPTER **28**

GOOD AND STRONG
AND BEAUTIFUL

YOU GAVE MRS. BROOK A SCARE,
Dad says.

What?

*She was very upset when she saw your fingers
scraped up like that.*

I was more upset. They're my fingers.

*I . . . understand you were trying to get some
quarter-cut oak.*

Yes and I Get It now. You were right. It's really not easy.

He sighs and looks at the sheet-covered chest in the corner for the first time ever and I want to start shaking my hands but I know that does not make Dad happy so I sit on them instead. My throat is sore and there is a double recess going on in my stomach but I say, *Dad. I want to finish the chest.*

I know, he says. But he doesn't say he will.

I want to get to Closure. Everything is starting to blur.

I know, he says even more quietly.

You need to get to Closure too.

This time he doesn't even say I know but he nods.

I think about what Devon would say. *You have to Work At It Dad. You have to try even if it's hard and you think you can never do it and you just want to scream and hide and shake your hands over and over and over.*

Dad wipes his eyes and I do too because mine are blurry and somehow I think it's really important to see right now. What I see is that his body is shaking which means he's crying and soon his voice comes out in strange-sounding gasps that sound like he is laughing weirdly or throwing up except nothing is coming out of his mouth. Finally he covers his face with his hands and stops the noise and his body stops shaking and after he sniffs twice he takes his hands away from his face and turns his head to me.

How did you get to be so smart?

I shrug. *I'm really working hard on finesse.*

Then he takes my hands in his and I don't even pull them away because he is looking at my cuts closely and I would want to do that too if I saw cuts on somebody's hands so I let him look.

Do you still really want to do this?

I don't know if he means to keep cutting the oak tree or work on the chest but I say, *Yes,* just in case he means the chest.

You think this will bring us Closure?

I shake my head. *No. I know it will.*

He blows a little air out of his nose and nods. He lets go of my hands and does one more big sigh. *Maybe we can make something good and strong and beautiful come out of this.*

Good and strong and beautiful. I like those words. They sound like Devon. I want to build something good and strong and beautiful.

Okay, Dad says. *Let's do it.*

YAY! I shout! *YAY DAD! YAY FOR ME! YAY FOR DEVON! LET'S START NOW!*

Dad puts his arms up like he's being arrested. *Okay. Okay.* This means quiet.

When can we start? I whisper.

First you need to learn a little about woodworking. We have some books—

I already read them! I shout because I forget to whisper.

You did?

Yes. You threw the books in Devon's room. Remember?

He nods. *Okay. You'll still need to do some hands-on learning. You have to do it and feel it to really Get It.*

Oh. Okay. I want to really Get It.

All right but it's bedtime now and we need a good sleep before working on it. We can start tomorrow.

First thing?

We'll need to get some supplies first.

Lowe's?

He nods.

They open at seven a.m. remember? When you and Devon used to work on the chest on weekends you got up early and—

I know.

We need to leave at six forty a.m. to get there in time and get a spot right by the door so we're first in line okay?

He sighs. *Okay.*

Do you want me to wake you up?

No. I can get up.

Are you sure?

Don't I get up on time every morning?

Yes. But what does that have to do with tomorrow morning?

I'll get up. Don't worry.

Okay but I'll wake you up if you're not up by six a.m. so you have time to shower.

After I go to bed I decide I should take the sheet off the chest to remind Dad we have to work on it but I have to stay up a long long time because Dad sits on the sofa forever just staring at the sheet. When he goes to bed I get up and go to the living room and take the sheet off the chest and I smile at all of its parts because we are finally going to have Closure.

And I hide the sheet inside my purple fleece and stuff it way under my bed where Dad can't find it in case he changes his mind.

CHAPTER **29**

PUTTING OUR LIFE BACK TOGETHER

I SHOW DAD DEVON'S LIST AND he nods. We go to Lowe's and get a lot of the supplies on the list including quarter-cut oak. We also buy things that aren't on the list. Like wood filler.

Before we can add anything to the chest Dad first has to put wood filler where the holes are from when he wrenched out the screws and threw the chest on the floor on The Day Our Life Fell Apart. He also has to cut out some sections that he destroyed when he kicked the chest on The Day Our Life Fell Apart. I think about those words and how I haven't said them lately. I think that maybe now is the day we start to put our life back together.

It takes Dad a long time to fix the parts that he broke. He scrunches up his face and makes noises like it hurts him as much as the chest. He even says, *This is rough,* and, *This is hard.*

I know, I say, after he says, *This is hard,* for the third time. *This is what happens when you have a TRM,* I tell him. *You make a mess. It's okay. You just have to try harder next time.*

I am trying hard, Dad says.

I know. You get a sticker.

Thank you.

Okay. You get another sticker for being polite.

Thanks. His lips press together and it almost looks like a smile. I forgot that Dad used to smile. I wonder if Closure will make him smile.

After a while Dad sits on the sofa and turns on Fox Five News.

You're not quitting are you? I ask him.

No. I'm just stuck. And I want to watch the news.

I don't like the news.

I'll only watch a little.

Is there any other way to get unstuck?

You can go get one of those woodworking books. It has the word Mission in the title. I need to take a look at it.

Okay. I run to Devon's room. I find the Mission book and start to leave but look back at the room. The sun is shining behind Devon's blue shade and I go back in to put his shade up so the sun pours in and makes his room warm and bright and I can see dust particles in the beams of light that maybe are part of Devon or maybe not but they make Devon's room look happy again.

Caitlin! Where's that book?

Coming! I say. But first I do something important. I leave Devon's door open.

When I come back in the living room the news lady is talking about the Virginia Dare shooter. *He was obviously disturbed,* she says, *just like the boys involved in today's school shooting in Maryland. Let me warn you that the video we are about to show of the event has some very disturbing content.*

Dad grabs the remote and shuts off the TV.

We both sit on the sofa without moving.

I hug the Mission book but it's not the same as my Dictionary. It doesn't take away the recess feeling in my stomach.

I would rather be under the sofa cushion than on top of it but I'm frozen in place.

We both look at the chest in the corner.

Dad sighs.

There is no face for Disturbed on the Facial Expressions Chart so I don't know exactly what it looks like. But I know it's not good. It's the kind of face that gives you a bad feeling because I thought everything would be okay now that we're working on the chest. But it's still not.

CHAPTER **30**

FRIENDS

OKAY, I TELL MRS. BROOK, *NOW it's soon. I'm ready.*

For what?

She doesn't Get It. *The whole friendship thing. It's time now.*

Oh Caitlin! Mrs. Brook claps. *I'm delighted! What changed your mind?*

Dad is working on the chest. It's hard for him. He really has to Work At It. If he can do it then I guess I can too. And also . . . maybe it really will help me get to Closure. The chest alone does not seem to be working.

I'm so proud of you!

I know.

I think you're really going to like this.

I shake my head. *I don't think I'm going to like it at all. I think it's going to hurt. But after the hurt I think maybe something good and strong and beautiful will come out of it.* Just like Dad said about the chest.

Mrs. Brook smiles so wide she has two rows of dimples. Her cheeks puff up and her eyes squish and water comes out of them and her face looks a little bit like a sponge.

At reading buddies time I manage not to scare my buddy. I keep my voice down. And I smile. Sometimes. I think it's a good start.

I do the special wave to Michael across the room. I think he grins even more than when Josh high-fives him which makes me feel very happy about how good I am at friendship.

In the cafeteria I sit down next to Laura who is very pretty and very popular. I think she should be my friend.

What are you doing? Laura asks.

Sitting next to you.

Why?

Because I want you to be my friend.

Laura looks at the people around her. They are all giggling and holding their trays but not sitting down. These are the girls who usually sit at Laura's table.

You can sit down, I tell them.

They look at each other and laugh or roll their eyes.

You're sitting where Anna sits, Laura says.

Oh, I say. It's nice of her to tell me because I honestly don't remember where every one of them sits. I take a bite of my cheese sandwich.

So move, Laura says. Her eyes are getting squishy and narrow.

I Look At The Person. *Where do you want me to sit?*

At a different table.

I take my tray and go to the table where I normally sit. Okay. That did not work. I can try someone else. But first I eat my sandwich because I'm hungry.

When I finish both halves I notice Mia at the next table.

She is not as pretty and not as popular as Laura but she could still be a good friend.

I go over to her and say, *Hi.*

Then I go back to my table and drink my juice box.

When I'm done I go say, *How are you?* to Mia because that's being polite.

O-kaaay, she says slowly.

I go back and sit down. Then I realize maybe she's not okay because her okay sounded kind of weird.

I go back to her. *Hi.*

She stares at me. So do Emma and some other girls who are with her. *What do you want?* Mia asks.

I want you to be my friend.

Like for today?

No. Forever.

I—I don't really know you.

That's okay. I can tell you what you need to know.

Um . . . I really just want to be alone. Mia starts giggling.

Emma frowns at her. *Mi-a!* she says in Dad's warning voice.

I can still Work At being a friend though because all

through lunch people keep coming up to Mia and bothering her. Every single time I go and tell those people, *Leave Mia alone. She wants to be alone today.*

Mia gets mad every time I have to say it. It doesn't make me mad though. I don't mind. I'm a good helper. And a good friend.

Finally Mia yells at me except I'm so surprised she's yelling at me that I don't even know what she says.

Emma comes into my Personal Space. *Caitlin. Um. Listen. You're really annoying Mia. You have to stop telling people to leave her alone.*

But she wants to be alone. She said so. I'm HELPING her.

Emma sighs. *You don't Get It. Mia doesn't really want everyone to leave her alone.*

Then why did she say that?

I guess she didn't want to hurt your feelings.

Why would that hurt my feelings?

Emma sighs again. *She wants YOU to leave her alone. Only you.*

Why?

Emma looks at the floor. *Well . . . because . . . she thinks you're . . . different.*

I think Emma is the one who doesn't Get It.

When we're in music Rachel throws up so Emma takes her to the school nurse. The teacher is busy trying to get someone to clean up the puke and everyone is saying, *Ew! P-U!* so I go over to Mia and ask her, *Why do you want me to leave you alone?*

Mia and the girls around her giggle. *Okay. Um. Because you're . . . special.*

Thank you, I say.

More giggles.

I mean, Mia says, *you're the kind of special that's a little weird.*

Weird?

Mia crosses her arms and breathes out LOUD. *Your behavior? You know?*

What do you mean? I ask.

She rolls her eyes. *Your behavior is . . . well . . . disturbing.*

Disturbing? My behavior is disturbing? The school shooter's behavior was disturbing. I start shaking my hands because that word is too scary and I can barely breathe.

She looks at my hands that are shaking faster and faster. *Yes. Disturbing.*

I am NOT disturbing!

You're disturbing us right now, one of the girls says. The rest of them start laughing.

Guys, guys! another girl says. *Stop it! Stop laughing! She's autistic. Like William H.*

My hands are shaking really fast now. *I am NOT autistic!*

Some of the girls laugh.

William doesn't talk. Can you HEAR ME TALKING?

Okay but—

William eats DIRT and SCREAMS when he gets mad! I AM NOT AUTISTIC! I am breathing hard and I want to jump out of my skin but I grit my teeth and shake my hands harder and turn and run away and I hear screaming and I don't know if it's music class or Mia or me.

I am sitting in Mrs. Brook's room staring at the table. *I thought special was good,* I mutter.

We're all special in different ways, she says. *Special IS good.*

Not if it's disturbing. How come she called me disturbing? And guess what? She disturbs me!

I can feel Mrs. Brook nodding even though I don't Look At The Person.

Besides, I tell her, *I'm NOT autistic. William H. is autistic.*

Caitlin, she says. *Did you know that William is very good at soccer? And that he can play the piano? And that he's my friend?*

No. I knew that he had Mrs. Brook time but I didn't know they were friends.

I like William, Mrs. Brook says. *And I can't play the piano at all or play soccer. We all have different talents—*

I know, I say.

But Mrs. Brook talks right on top of my words—*and just because we're better at some things than William doesn't mean we're any better than he is.*

I didn't say that.

But it sounds like that's what you meant.

I nod and sigh. *It is what I meant.*

Do you see how it's not fair for you to—

Yes, I say. It's my turn to talk on top of her words now. *I Get It. William H. even remembers to smile a lot more than I do so there are several things he's better at than me.* I sigh again. *But I'm still not like him. Not exactly.* I Look At The Person. *Am I?*

We all fall on the spectrum of behavior somewhere. She

puts one hand on one side of the table and her other grips the far side. *Here's the spectrum,* she says. *It's a line and we're all on it. Some of us are farther along the line than others.*

I know from art class that a spectrum is all the colors of the rainbow. It's more like a prism than a line. Or maybe a fat line with lots of colors. I don't like the way colors blur together in art. How do you know where one ends and the other begins? I have to know exactly where I am in space. That's why I draw in black and white.

Mrs. Brook picks up one hand and runs a finger almost all the way to the end of the table. *You're around here. Very high functioning. Very smart. Very capable.*

William H. is on the other side, I say.

William is farther along the line. Yes.

I grip the edges of the table like Mrs. Brook and squinch my eyes at the tabletop and wonder which spot EXACTLY is me. I don't want to run into anyone else. You just don't know what might happen.

Are you feeling better now Caitlin?

I think I'll skip the friend thing.

You should be very proud of yourself for trying so hard today. Remember that everyone can find a friend. She is still gripping the edges of the table. So hard that her knuckles are pale. *And obviously we need to work on friendship skills in the fifth grade as a whole. These girls need some educating.*

They need to learn some finesse too, I say.

Mrs. Brook nods. *Yes. And some better friendship skills.*

I know it. They will never make friends that way.

CHAPTER 31

IT'S A GIRL THING

AFTER RECESS I HATE PE THE most. Recess I hate because everyone screams and runs around crazy and grabs you and pushes you and you have absolutely no idea what will happen next. At least in PE there is a teacher so you know what will happen next even though it might involve screaming, grabbing and running around crazy.

Class! Mr. Mason shouts. He always shouts. It's just what PE teachers do. *Boys! JoshNelson-*

BruceShaneJoey! Stop that right now or you'll be getting a special one-way ticket to see Miss Harper!

I don't see why they get to have a special one-way ticket to the principal's office. I'm behaving myself perfectly and I am getting no free tickets.

I'm breaking you boys up! Josh—Josh! You and Nelson are on that side of the gym and the rest of you hooligans are on this side! Shane and Bruce! You're in charge of William H. His assistant isn't here today. Make sure he doesn't run off if I turn my back!

Can we have free play today? a boy asks.

When pigs fly, Mr. Mason says. I'm not sure what he means by that.

Dodgeball today! he yells, and I start sucking on my sleeve. Dodgeball is bad enough but I hope he doesn't try to make us wear pinnies. I hate the feel of them. And they remind me of clamshells and I hate the gooey icky inside of a clam.

He goes to the closet and pulls out the big cardboard box with the pinnies and I start sucking both sleeves. He grabs William H. who is trying to run out the door. *Shane and Bruce! What did I just tell you? You're watching William H.!*

Everyone else—put on these pinnies! And hurry! William H. loves dodgeball so the sooner we get this game started the better!

Mr. Mason starts throwing yellow and red pinnies at people around the gym.

A yellow one lands at my feet and I stare at it.

Come on Caitlin! Pick it up!

I stare at it.

What's the problem!

I don't like clams.

Me neither! Put on the pinnie!

Mr. Mason! Shane yells. *I can't hold William H.!*

Mr. Mason swears and goes to grab William H. *Hurry up and get ready!* He looks over at me. *Caitlin! The pinnie!*

But I don't like clams.

What's that got to do with the price of fish!

What? Why is he talking about fish?

Oh for the love of— Why do they give me all the autistic kids?

Some people laugh. I'm not sure who all the autistic kids are. I thought William H. was the only one.

Some girls are whispering next to me. I brace myself because when a bunch of girls is whispering that usually means someone will squeal or scream so I need to be prepared. Emma is one of the girls and she's pretty loud most of the time.

This time is no different. She tells Mr. Mason, *Some of us need to go see Mrs. Brook.*

Why? Mr. Mason asks.

I wonder too. I never knew she went to see Mrs. Brook.

The other girls are also looking at her. Finally she answers. *It's a girl thing.*

Mr. Mason's face goes red and he nods.

I will have to remember that remark.

Emma looks at me then at Mr. Mason then back to me. *I think you should come with us.*

I follow Emma and two other girls down the hall to Mrs. Brook's room. Emma is complaining loudly about Mr. Mason, saying, *That was SO inappropriate,* even though there's No Talking In The Hall. I try to remind her but Emma's voice takes up all the room. When she grows up she should be one of those TV interviewers on Fox Five News who doesn't let anyone else talk even if they try.

When we get to Mrs. Brook's room she's on the phone

but it doesn't stop Emma from blurting out something so fast I can't even follow it.

Mrs. Brook tells the phone person she'll have to call back and she hangs up.

What happened? Mrs. Brook asks.

No one says anything.

What exactly did Mr. Mason say?

Still no one says anything.

Then they all look at me.

This means they want me to tell Mrs. Brook what happened.

So I do. *Mr. Mason wants to know why they give him all the autistic kids.*

Mrs. Brook's neck does its turtle jerk. She looks at the girls. *I see.*

I look at Emma and the other two girls also. *I don't think they're autistic. I don't know who he's talking about.*

Emma looks at me with a sad face. *He was talking about you.*

But I'M NOT—

I know, she says quickly. *He shouldn't have said that.*

He knows that too, Mrs. Brook says. *We're all still . . . very stressed.*

One of the other girls says, *William H. doesn't have his assistant so Mr. Mason is going a little nuts.*

Oh dear! Mrs. Brook stands up. *Someone should have told me!*

Her shoes squeak down the hall to the gym very fast and we follow. She speaks with Mr. Mason and takes William H. from Bruce and Shane.

Mr. Mason comes over to me.

I think he's going to make me wear the pinnie so I start to talk but he interrupts me.

I'm really sorry Caitlin. I shouldn't have said that remark about autistic kids.

I'm surprised to hear him speak without shouting. *That's okay. I think William H. is the only autistic kid they give you though.*

You're right Caitlin. He sighs. *I learned a good lesson today.*

Do I have to wear the pinnie?

He smiles. *You know what? Today I think I have to wear*

the pinnie. He goes to the box and puts on a yellow pinnie but it only fits around his neck instead of his whole body and it looks like a scarf. People laugh at him but he laughs too. He also winks at me. And even though he looks funny I think he has learned a little finesse today.

CHAPTER **32**

DAD-OH

WHAT IS A DAD-OH? I ASK DAD.

DAY-doe, he says, *and it's a groove in a piece of wood.* But his lip curls up on one side.

He is starting to smile. I know what that means. Closure must be coming!

So I Work At It. *I like DAD-OH better.*

His lips curl up again on the left side.

I say Dad-oh four more times.

Here is the screwdriver Dad-oh.

Would you like a glass of water Dad-oh?

What do we do next Dad-oh?

Can I help you Dad-oh?

And his lips curl up on the left side every time.

And when I say it one more time, *Good night Dad-oh,* both sides of his lips curl up. So do mine. Because Closure is a very good thing to see.

After Dad-oh goes to bed and I'm sure he's asleep I sneak into Devon's room and borrow his Boy Scout knife and camping flashlight and go to the living room. Then I slide my head under the chest and turn on the flashlight so it lights up just the bottom of the chest. That way the room stays dark and Dad won't know what I'm doing. I look for the perfect spot on the underside of the chest and I carve in big letters on his chest just like Devon did for me: SCOUT.

CHAPTER **33**

GROUP PROJECT INCLUDING OTHER PEOPLE

MRS. JOHNSON ANNOUNCES AN-other group project. I raise my hand. She closes her eyes for a moment and sighs. *Yes Caitlin. I know you don't want to be in a group but—*

I do want to be in a group. This is going to be my first group project in a group. I add, *In school,* because I remember that the chest is kind of a group project with Dad-oh.

Oh. Okay. That's great. She claps twice. *Class! We're going to the computer lab so you can do your research. We have to share the computers with the other fifth-grade class so some of you will need to sit at the tables.*

Some people groan. I don't. I just think one thing. Josh.

We're lucky to have a computer lab at all in such a small school, Mrs. Johnson reminds us like she does every time we go to the computer lab. *I'm going to bring some supplies with us and when we get there we'll break into groups and I'll tell you what the project is.*

We all get up and I see Mrs. Johnson pick up two bins of markers which is a very good sign. It means there is drawing involved.

At the computer lab Mrs. Johnson says, *Our project is on the state of Virginia. It's a project that involves research and a lot of drawing because you'll need the flag, the state flower, the state bird, et cetera.*

I'm so happy! I love drawing!

Emma invites me to join her group with Brianna and

Shane. *Okay,* I say, and I tell them how lucky they are. *I'm probably the best artist in the state of Virginia.*

Shane and Brianna look at each other and laugh. I wonder if they're happy.

Emma chews her lip. *You don't have to be the best. You can do all the drawing though if you want.*

Yay! I smile at my group until my cheeks start hurting and I have to stop.

Mrs. Johnson puts markers and paper and some books about Virginia on the tables. Shane wants to sit at the computer so I sit next to Emma and Brianna at one of the tables in the back of the room with a bunch of kids from the other fifth grade. Josh is at the table in front of ours. I don't look at him. I start drawing right away.

Hey! You! Josh says.

I want to shake my hands but instead I draw even faster.

Emma whips her head up from the book she's reading. *Shut up Josh!*

His face goes pink and his eyes blink a lot. *I was just going to see if I could borrow a red marker. Thanks a lot!* He turns around and sniffs.

I stop drawing and look down at my pile of markers next to me. There are three red ones. I take one and lean across the table and poke Josh in the back with it.

He whirls around. *What the—!*

Here, I say.

His lips squish around a lot so I can't tell if he's smiling or frowning but he takes the marker from me. He does not say thank you but I decide I'll accept his thank you from earlier.

Shane looks up the state everything on the computer. *The state dog is the American foxhound and the state fish is a brook trout,* he calls out.

I draw them and also a dogwood—the state tree AND flower—with a cardinal in it—the state bird. Everyone thinks cardinals are red but actually that's just the male. I don't do colors so my cardinal is a female. When I'm done I show my group.

Brianna shakes her head. *You traced that.*

No I didn't.

No one can draw like that.

I can. I told you. I'm probably the best artist in the state.

Yeah right.

I've seen what Caitlin can draw, Emma says. *It's awesome. And anyway it doesn't matter. It can be traced or drawn for this project.*

I drew it, I tell her.

Whatever, Brianna says.

Can you make the cardinal red? Emma asks.

I don't do colors, I tell her.

Why not?

It's easier when things are black and white.

But you've done the hard part already, Emma says. *Coloring something in is easy. It's drawing the tree and bird that's hard.*

Not for me, I say. *Colors are mushy and I don't know where they end or what happens to them when they run into each other because they change.*

Emma tilts her head. *I don't Get It. Black and white is boring. Colors are beautiful.*

I take a deep breath and try to explain. *When you mix red and yellow it might come out orange like the sun when it's setting but when you mix red and yellow another time it might*

193

come out like a school bus and when you do it again it might come out like a hornet. It's always different. You don't know what to expect.

Emma's head is still tilted. And she's not saying anything. Which means she REALLY doesn't Get It because it's unusual for Emma not to talk.

Never mind, I tell her. *It's too hard to explain.* I'm not even sure I Get It myself.

I get to see Michael on the playground and talk to him for the first time in what feels like a really long time. I tell him all about the chest Dad-oh and I are working on.

He listens politely but his Bambi eyes are kind of fuzzy.

What's wrong? I ask him.

I don't Get It.

So I describe the chest and exactly what we're doing to it and how it'll look when we're finished.

I still don't Get It, he says.

I start describing the chest again.

No. I mean I don't Get how that makes Closure.

We're bringing the project to Closure. We're finishing the chest. That's Closure.

Oh. But his eyes are still fuzzy. *Will I feel better when it's done?*

I think about it for a minute. I'm pretty sure I'll feel better. Much better than seeing it covered by a gray sheet in the corner. And I think Dad will feel better too. I know Devon would want it finished. I look at Michael with his fuzzy Bambi eyes and I'm not so sure how finishing the chest will help him. And it's giving me a recess feeling in my stomach.

He shrugs. *That's okay.*

But it doesn't sound okay. And my stomach doesn't feel okay.

You're still my friend, he says softly.

I am? Why?

You're nice to me and you don't have to be 'cause you're a fifth grader and you can do stuff like Closure and I'm only a first grader so I can only do stuff like be a pear.

A pair of what?

No. A pear. Like an apple.

Oh. Can I see you be a pear?

He Looks At The Person. *You really want to see me be a pear?*

Yes.

He starts to smile. *You want to come to my play?*

What play?

My class is doing a play about the food pyramid. I'm the pear. It's my favorite fruit. Do you want to come watch?

When is it?

Tonight. At school. Can you come?

I don't like going back to school once I'm already home. It's like having school twice in one day. But Michael is finally looking happy so I decide the answer should be, *Okay.*

My teacher said you have to be here with your costume by six thirty sharp. Oh. Except you don't have to get here until seven because you're one of the watchers.

Audience, I say.

Michael gives me a high five and he's smiling so much that I feel like a good friend again. I'm happy because of Michael. He's the only friend I have and maybe the only friend I'll ever have.

CHAPTER **34**

MICHAEL'S PLAY

THAT NIGHT WHEN WE'RE WORK-
ing on the chest I tell Dad, *I have to go to school
tonight.*

Tonight? What for?

Michael is in a play.

Who's Michael?

My friend.

Your friend? Do I know him?

I shrug and wonder how I'm supposed to
know that. *He's in first grade,* I tell him.

And he's your friend?

Yes. So I HAVE to go to his play. It's important. It's at seven o'clock.

Dad looks at his watch. *It's almost quarter to seven already.*

I stand up fast. *Then we have to go NOW because it takes almost nine minutes to get to school.*

Caitlin—

I don't want to be LATE.

You should've told me before—

It is before. But we have to MOVE!

I wasn't planning on going out tonight.

You don't have to plan! It's already planned!

I run to the door and open it. *I'll be IN THE CAR!* I run across the grass and pull on the car door but it won't open. I run around to all four doors. They are all locked. *IT'S LOCKED IT'S LOCKED IT'S LOCKED IT'S LOCKED!*

I hear the front door slam and Dad's shoes clomping fast. *I'M COMING!*

HURRY! HURRY!

The car beeps. The lights turn on and I open the door and throw myself inside.

Dad gets in the front seat and turns on the engine.

DRIVE! DRIVE!

He makes the engine go LOUD and whips around to me. I'm glad there is a seat back between us because he is trying to get into my Personal Space.

Caitlin! I'm not happy about this. Next time I need some warning—

I'M WARNING YOU! I say in my warning voice.

CAITLIN!

DRIVE! DRIVE! FAST! NOW!

He lurches out of the driveway and I'm thrown off the backseat.

PUT ON YOUR SEAT BELT! he yells.

DON'T YELL! I HATE IT WHEN PEOPLE YELL!

Dad mutters a lot of things but I can't hear them and I don't care because at least he's not yelling.

What time is it NOW Dad?

We have plenty of time.

WHAT TIME IS IT?

IT'S—he stops and takes a breath—*it's six forty-eight.*

We'll get there at six fifty-seven. Unless you HURRY then maybe we can get there at six fifty-six. Then we have to park and walk inside.

Where is the play?

I TOLD YOU! At SCHOOL!

I know, he hisses, *but where in the school?*

I freeze. Cafeteria? Gym? Classroom? *I DON'T KNOW! OH NOOOOO!*

Dad switches to his Nice Voice fast. *We'll find it. It's okay. It's okay. And we'll get there in plenty of time. No problem. You'll see Michael. And Michael will be happy to see you. It's great to have a friend. Isn't it? I'm really proud of you.*

He keeps talking but I don't listen. I just moan and chew and suck my sleeve until we pull into the school and he says, *Ahh the lights are on in the cafeteria and lots of people and little kids are there so that's where it is. You see? Everything is okay.*

Dad pulls into a Handicapped Spot right by the cafeteria door and I tell him, *You can't park here,* but he turns off the engine and opens his door and says, *This counts.*

He opens my door and says, *Come on. We made it.*

There is no place left to sit where I can actually see Michael who is dressed in a smashed cardboard box that's painted yellow to look like a pear. Sort of. I have to stand against the wall by the OUT door. I hate standing up. It makes my feet hurt. And I can smell the wet cafeteria smell and the lights are too bright.

At least I'm farther away from the noisy people. They are all talking LOUD about anything. I hear security system and school board and babysitter and nightmares and ulcer and high fiber. Not one person says food pyramid or dairy product or candy or anything about why they are here. They are worse than my class because most of the time we at least know what the subject is. They might as well go home if they don't want to be here. That's what Mrs. Johnson says.

Finally Mrs. Hanratty the kindergarten teacher gets up and tells everyone about healthy eating and the play begins and the people finally focus—their cameras at least.

Michael looks around the room and I know he is looking for me so I raise my hand high and close and open it three times and then six before he notices and waves back with a big grin on his face.

Afterward I tell Michael he looks like a pear even though he looks more like a kid in a squished cardboard box. The part about the squished box I just think in my head.

I think that makes him happy because he smiles. And he says, *You're like my big sister.*

It makes me feel kind of warm and glowy on the inside.

Wait here! he says, and is back a moment later dragging a man. *This is my dad.*

You must be Caitlin. It's great to meet you. I've heard so much about you, Michael's dad says.

I don't like football, I tell him.

Oh, he says.

But it's okay if you do. I remember to smile.

Thank you! He smiles at me too and so does Michael.

Then Dad and Michael's dad talk for a long time while Michael and I try to make the food pyramid out of all the snacks. It's really hard to get brownies to balance on top of carrot sticks though.

On the drive home I think about Michael being dressed up as a pear and how that's better than having to dress up as a ham like Scout did in *To Kill a Mockingbird*.

I ask Dad, *Do you remember that movie?*

What movie?

To Kill a Mockingbird.

Oh. Yes I do.

It's a good one isn't it?

It's been a long time since I've seen it but it was one of the best.

Devon liked it too.

Dad clears his throat and his hands clench and unclench the steering wheel. *Yes he did.*

Do you think I'm like Scout?

The little girl in the movie? Dad nods. Then he also says, *Very much.*

I grin. *You're like Atticus. He was brave.*

Thank you. He sighs. *I wish I were more like Atticus.*

Being like Scout makes me happy so I want him to feel just like Atticus. *Maybe you can get glasses like his.*

If I ever need glasses I'll think about buying some like his.

Maybe you should dress like him.

I'm not sure. His clothes are too practical for my kind of job.

Maybe you can shoot a dog.

We swerve on the road a little. *I'd rather not do that.*

Just one that was going to kill us. A sick dog. Can I get some overalls like Scout?

Honey . . . we have to live in the real world. I like you as Caitlin.

But you said the movie was the best.

For a movie. But this is real life. A movie isn't as good as real life. It can't even compare.

Dad is wrong about that. A movie is better than real life because in the movies only the bad guys die. Or you can pick the good movies where the bad guys die and only watch those. If you get tricked and a good person dies in the movie then you can rewrite it in your head so the good person lives and the part about death is superfluous.

Right honey?

Dad has been talking but I wasn't ready to listen. *What?*

Life is special.

You mean . . . it's not just me who's special? It's all of life?

Yes.

I guess the good news is that everybody has to put up with being special because everybody is alive.

CHAPTER 35

MONKEY BARS

ON MONDAY WE HAVE A FIRE drill which means first recess is late so they get to stay out for part of second recess. I don't like that many kids at once. That many kids can only lead to problems which is exactly what happens. Mrs. Brook has to take three boys inside who get in a big fight.

I look around for Michael. I still feel warm and fuzzy because I'm his big sister. I'll take care of him just like Devon always took care of me. Scout's honor.

And then I see Michael and my hands start shaking.

He is on the monkey bars.

He is screaming.

And Josh is pulling on his legs.

NOOOOOOOO! I run all the way to the monkey bars and I HIT Josh hard and yell, *LET GO OF HIM! LEAVE HIM ALONE! DON'T TOUCH HIM! YOU'RE EVIL!*

Stop hitting me you freak! Josh yells.

But I have to keep hitting him because he won't let go of Michael.

Stop! Stop! Michael says. *And don't call my friend a freak!*

I'm helping him stay up, Josh says as I try to pry his hands off of Michael.

No you're not! I say. *You're evil Evil EVIL!*

Stop it or I'll fall! Michael screams.

Josh lets go. *You idiot!* he says to me.

Don't say that! Michael shouts.

Josh's face is red. *Can't you see I'm trying to help?*

You're evil! I say.

Help! I'm going to fall! Michael screams. *Somebody catch me!*

Josh steps under Michael before I can stop him and I watch as Michael falls into his arms diagonally and Josh puts him upright and sets him carefully on the ground.

Josh looks at Michael then at me. His face is swollen and his voice cracks even though he only has one word to say. *See?*

Josh was helping me, Michael says.

Oh, I say.

No kidding? somebody asks.

I look around and there are a bunch of kids around the monkey bars now staring at Josh. I think Josh has just noticed them too. He steps back from the crowd.

Why does everyone think I'm bad? Josh's voice is a whisper.

I don't, Michael says, but his voice is covered up by the crowd talking.

Because you are, a boy says LOUD. *Duh!*

You're mean, someone else says.

Yeah Josh, a voice shouts. *It runs in your family.*

Ooooh, a lot of people say.

I'm not like my cousin! Josh shouts. *It's not fair! Everyone blames me!* He looks at the crowd.

They do? I say.

Yes! Everyone hates me because he killed those people. YOU hate me because of that!

I shake my head. *No. I hate you because you're mean to people. Except I guess you're nice to Michael. I wish you'd make up your mind and be mean or be nice. Then I'd know how to feel.*

I'm mean to people because they're mean to me!

Oh. Well maybe if you're nice to people they'll be nice to you, I tell him.

Michael pulls Josh's sleeve. *I like you Josh. You read to me and you give me high fives and you stopped Avery when he was pushing me and you helped me up on the monkey bars and you promised you wouldn't let me fall and you didn't. You caught me Josh.*

I don't know why this is a reason to cry but Josh drops on his knees and covers his face. I can hear him crying behind his hands though.

The crowd is quiet now. Nobody says anything.

Michael kneels down next to Josh and pats his back. *Caitlin thought you were trying to hurt me because sometimes you pull people off the monkey bars.*

Josh is still sobbing. He stretches his hands so his palms cover his eyes and his fingers are covering the top of his head. It looks like he's trying to cover his whole head but it's not working. I watch him and I wonder if he wants a fleece or a sofa cushion to cover him up. That's what I want when I feel bad.

Michael looks up at me with his Bambi eyes. In them I see sadness and I think it's fear or maybe it's confusion. I also see friendship. And I think there's a look that means I need to do something to help. To answer the question. I think it's the look I gave Devon. A lot.

So I kneel down on the other side of Josh and pat his back too and tell him it's okay the same way Devon used to tell me and Dad still tells me. The way that I can really believe it. And if this is empathy I hope Josh can feel some of the empathy that's starting to come out of me.

CHAPTER **36**

MORE DRAWING

OUR GROUP PROJECT IS DONE and we have to present it to the class. Emma does all the talking and I hold up my drawings so I can hide my face behind them. Mrs. Johnson and a lot of people say, *Wow! That's an awesome bird! Look at that dog! She can really draw!* and nice things like that but this way I don't have to Look At The Person. Also I don't even have to say Thank You because Emma is trying to talk and it would be rude for me to talk at the same time.

The class claps. Mrs. Johnson gives us an A. She puts all of my drawings on the bulletin board and I feel happy until she puts other people's drawings up and theirs are all in color. Now mine don't look as good somehow. I stare at mine and wonder how they would look with color even though I like things better without color. I think.

Emma says that our group should sit at lunch together so we do. Shane shrugs. Brianna rolls her eyes. I eat my cheese crackers and chocolate milk and fruit leather strip.

Could you chew with your mouth closed please? Brianna asks. Her eyes are big and so is her voice. I'm confused. I'm not sure who she's talking to.

Do you mean me? I ask her.

Yes! And don't talk with your mouth full! she says.

Shane snorts.

I'm serious! Brianna says.

Caitlin, Emma says after she swallows a bite of her hot dog, *can you do some drawings for the yearbook?*

I don't know, I say. *What kind of drawings?*

Her forehead wrinkles. *I think drawings in the margins would be good. They could be of things around school.*

I think of what's around school. *The grass?*

No. Not just grass.

The street?

No. I mean things you see in the classroom or out on the playground. Books. Computers. Desks. Monkey bars. School stuff.

I nod slowly. *I could do that.*

High five, Emma says. She puts her hand in the air.

I look at it and think about how Michael and Josh high-five.

I put my hand up and Emma slaps it.

It feels weird but in a good way.

You should join the art club in middle school, she says.

There's an art club?

Sure! Mr. Walters runs it. He's the art teacher.

I know Mr. Walters.

He's cool, Emma says.

I nod. *I need to draw his eyes.*

She shrugs and grins. *Okay.*

At home our chest is almost done.

I draw what I want to carve into the top part of it. The bird is gray and black and white and has a long tail. Her head is tilted up and her beak is open like she's singing. She is beautiful. I'm happy because I get my drawing just right. I run to the living room to show it to Dad.

He takes it with one hand and rubs his chin with the other. He sits down on the sofa with an oof. He stares at it. *It's not . . . It doesn't look as . . . detailed as that eagle you drew that won first prize.*

It's not an eagle, I tell him. *It's a mockingbird.*

He tilts his head to the side and stares at me. *I thought it was an eagle because this is Devon's Eagle Scout project.*

It's a mockingbird, I explain, *like in the movie. Remember? Because Devon was like Jem. And I'm like Scout. And you Dad—you're like Atticus.*

Dad's eyes fill with water and he blinks a lot and I think maybe he needs to get those funny glasses Atticus wears.

CHAPTER 37

NO MORE VIRGINIA DARE

I'M PROUD WHEN I TELL MRS.
Brook the chest is done. I also tell her that I
have one really good friend which is Michael
and one sort of maybe future friend which is
Emma. And maybe Mr. Walters.

Mrs. Brook smiles. *Do you think you're coming to Closure?*

I think so.

How about your dad?

I think working on the chest helped him too.

I'm very glad you came up with that idea, she says.

I smile because I'm glad too. But then I frown.

What's wrong?

I don't think I've gotten Closure for Michael.

She sighs. *A lot of people still need to find Closure.*

Who else?

The whole community Caitlin—especially the students and teachers at Virginia Dare Middle School. Oh! Did you hear? The school board voted to change the school name over the summer.

Why?

There are a lot of bad memories associated with that name. I think they're trying to find Closure too.

I'm not sure I Get It but I try to figure it out. It doesn't work. *I don't see how changing the name is going to bring Closure.*

No. But it's a step. Maybe you can come up with something else.

Me? Why me?

Because you're going there next year. It's part of your community.

Suddenly I don't feel so proud anymore. I still need to find Closure for Michael AND I have to find Closure for a whole entire school. And now the community too? How am I going to do all that?

CHAPTER **38**

I GET IT

CLOSURE WASN'T SUPPOSED TO feel sad like this.

That night after Dad goes to bed I stay up and stare at the finished chest. Even though it's finished there's still something missing and I have to Work At It to figure out what it is. I think Dad is mostly happy that it's completed and beautiful. I'm mostly happy too. But the chest isn't helping Michael or the people of the middle school that's getting a new name this summer or the rest of the whole entire community. I have to figure that out because that's part of empathy. Even though I didn't think I'd like empathy it kind of creeps up on you and makes you feel all warm and glowy inside. I don't think I want to go back to life without empathy.

I put my head under the sofa cushion and stare at the chest so I can think of an answer but instead I think of Devon and I wish he were here so he could tell me the answer and I think about how he can never tell me anything or do anything again—not ride his bike or play baseball or watch *To Kill a Mockingbird* or be an Eagle Scout.

I hear the crying and then I see Dad's hand reaching under the sofa cushion and pushing the wet hair out of my eyes. But I can't stop crying. For Devon. Because of what happened to Devon. Because his life got taken away and he can't do anything and he can't be happy or proud or live or love—and all of a sudden my gulp-crying turns into gulp-laughing because I realize something.

Dad-oh! Dad! Oh Dad! I cry.

What is it Caitlin?

Devon, I cry, *Devon.*

I know. It hurts. You miss him. I miss him.

No, I say, *Devon!*

I know, he says.

But I'm not crying for ME! I pull my head out from under the sofa cushion and Look At The Person. *I'm crying for Devon! I'm crying because I feel bad for HIM! Isn't that empathy? I'm feeling for HIM instead of me!*

Dad smiles even though he has crying eyes. *Yes,* he says, *yes. Now you know what it's like to feel for other people.*

He hugs me and we sit together for a long time on the sofa. Empathy isn't as hard as it sounds because people have a lot of the same feelings. And it helps to understand other people because then you can actually care about them sometimes. And help them. And have a friend. Like Michael. And do something for them and make them feel as good as you're feeling.

I look over at Devon's chest and it makes me feel good. *We did a great job on it,* I say, *didn't we Dad?*

Yes we did.

We made something good and strong and beautiful.

He nods. *We sure did. Devon would be very proud.*

I nod too. I think about Devon and how he would show

it to all the Scouts and tell everyone how we made it and how we used it to find Closure. And when I'm staring at the Mockingbird and seeing her mouth looking up like she's telling the whole world something THAT'S when I feel my mouth turn into a grin and my hands start shaking so hard I have to leap off the sofa and jump around the room because just shaking my hands isn't enough for all the excitement because I finally Get It! I Get It! I GET IT!

C HAPTER **39**

COLORS

I DON'T LIKE THE BRIGHT LIGHTS of the middle school auditorium or the loud whispering all around us or having to wear these itchy clothes and I especially don't like being in the front row with everyone staring at me. Dad said the smiling bald man onstage is the principal but I don't like him either because he keeps pressing buttons on the microphone making it crackle LOUD and I wish he would stop it. The noise keeps making me want to jump out of my seat and I can't hold myself down because Dad is sitting next to me grabbing both armrests already so I can't use the one near me. I put both my hands on the armrest on the other side and try hard not to moan very loud. It must be working because Dad is not telling me to stop. He just sits there with his lips squeezed tight and his fists on the armrests and he stares at the stage.

I look at the stage too. It's wooden and has dark blue curtains because the middle school colors are blue and white. There's a big blue curtain at the back of the stage so you can't see what's behind there. And a big shape that's partly covered by the same blue fabric except its feet and pedals are sticking out so I know it's a piano. I know this place already. I've been here about fifty times. The Scouts had all their ceremonies here. Most of the time I even sat in this seat.

There are several chairs onstage with seats and backs also in dark blue cloth. Mrs. Brook is sitting on the chair at the end and tapping another blue cloth shape with the index card she's holding. Her lips are moving and I guess she's reading the card. It's her speech. I'm glad she's giving the speech and not me. I'm nervous enough. My Heart is going *POUND-POUND-POUND*.

Hi Caitlin.

I jump. Then I see it's Michael.

He sits down on the other side of me. *Are you ready?*

Ready? My hands start shaking so I sit on them. *I don't have to do anything.*

I know. He grins. *You already did.*

Hello Caitlin, Michael's dad says. He waves from a few seats away because Josh is sitting on the other side of Michael. Josh is all dressed up in a suit like he's going to church. He says, *Hi,* too but he doesn't Look At The Person.

I don't really mind that Josh is sitting on the other side of Michael because even though he's not my favorite person he is nice to Michael. I take two gummy worms out of my pocket and give them to Michael.

He smiles. *This one's Caitlin and this one's Josh.*

When he says Josh's name I remember that Josh is Michael's friend. So I offer him a gummy worm too.

Josh stares at it until Michael elbows him.

Slowly Josh reaches his hand out and takes it from me. He even Looks At The Person this time. *Thanks.*

You're welcome.

Michael grins and whispers to me, *Good remembering Your Manners.*

I nod. I don't even need the chart anymore. Not now that I know they're MY manners and I can do whatever I want with them.

The microphone squawks and I jump again. *We'll give people just a couple more minutes to find their seats,* the principal says, *then we'll begin the ceremony.*

Hey Caitlin, Michael says, but his dad says, *Shhh! Michael. It's time to settle down.* Then Mr. Schneider points up at the stage and Michael looks there too. So do I.

I see the principal walk over to the left side of the stage where Mrs. Brook is sitting and I think he's going to walk down the steps and I hold my breath but instead he touches the blue fabric next to Mrs. Brook and talks to her.

I let out my breath slowly but I can't help looking at those worn wooden steps on the left side of the room that go up to the stage. And I start shaking. Those steps scare me. They creak LOUD. Especially when the auditorium is quiet. The third step is the worst. I know. When Devon walked up the steps to get his Life rank the whole auditorium was silent because like Dad said it's a big event for a seventh grader to get his Life rank so soon. But when Devon put his weight on the third step it creaked so loud it sounded like a gun went off and it scared me so I screamed and then everyone stared at me and started whispering and a little kid even pointed at me and said, *It was her!* And I started crying. Devon jumped off the steps and came running over to me saying, *It's okay. It's okay.* But it didn't feel okay even when he tried to give me a gummy worm because I had a recess feeling in my stomach and I didn't want it. He held my hand even though it was shaking up and down and he tried to get me to go up onstage with him but I didn't want to get anywhere near that step but mostly I didn't want to stand up in front of everyone because they were all staring at me so I pulled my hand away from his and said, *No no no!* And he said, *Everything's okay. Just watch me. I'll be up there,* and he pointed to where Dad was standing onstage and I didn't answer him so he said, *See?* And I still wouldn't answer him so he said, *I have to go now Scout. I'll be up there. You're going to be just fine.*

I have a recess feeling in my tummy now. All I see is fuzzy blue because my eyes are blurring everything together. I wish it were the blue of Devon's room and I were in my hidey-hole with my purple fleece looking up at the carving of my name. SCOUT.

The microphone squawks and I jump again. *Welcome!* the principal says. *Welcome everyone. Thank you for coming to this very special dedication ceremony.*

I'm not sure I want to hear everything he says so while he's talking I keep stuffed-animaling and I just hear certain words like *healing* and *coming together* and *community*. When he says *Closure* everything stops and I blink and look up at him and I squint because the stage lights are so bright and his bald head is reflecting the light like the sun.

He takes a deep breath. The microphone crackles. He flips over the piece of paper he's holding and it hits the microphone with a pop. Then there's silence.

Let me read the names, he says.

I close my eyes.

He speaks slowly but loudly. *Julianne Denise Morris.*

There's a murmuring in the crowd for a moment until it's quiet again.

Roberta L. Schneider, the principal says.

I hear Michael beside me. *Mommy,* he says. *That's my mommy.*

I look over at him and he's staring up at the principal with his Bambi eyes.

Mr. Schneider is blinking and covering his mouth with his hand.

And I hear the next name. *Devon. Joseph. Smith.*

My Heart that has been pounding this whole time suddenly seems to stop.

I hear Dad swallow.

The auditorium is silent except for the rustling of the principal's jacket as he turns away from the microphone and then the slow *squeak squeak squeak* of his shoes as he walks over to Mrs. Brook's side of the stage. He puts his hand on the blue fabric shape and turns to face the audience. And he starts to speak. Even though he doesn't have a microphone his voice booms across the auditorium.

This beautiful Mission-style chest was started by Devon for his Eagle Scout project—his voice stops for a moment—*and then finished and donated to our middle school by his beloved father. Harold Joseph Smith. And his little sister whom he adored. Caitlin.*

The principal pulls the fabric off of the shape like he's a magician and everyone says, *Oh!* and, *Ah!*

And there it is.

Devon's chest.

With SCOUT carved and hidden underneath.

And the Mockingbird on top that I can't see from here but I know it's there.

His chest is good and strong and beautiful. Just like Devon.

Everyone is clapping. Even Josh. Dad blows his nose and wipes his eyes but he's smiling. The clapping is so loud it hurts my ears but it's a good hurt and I feel the crowd looking at me but it's not in a bad way so I don't mind so much.

Michael smiles and points at me and says, *It was her!* and I don't mind that either because he's happy and I'm glad that Devon's chest is bringing him Closure too.

Mrs. Brook is at the podium and she talks but I don't know what she says until I hear her talking to me. *Caitlin. Caitlin! Please stand up. I think everyone wants to see you.* She smiles at me.

So I stand up but I don't turn around and look at the audience because I want to see—really see—the Mockingbird on Devon's chest so I stand on my tiptoes and stare at it. I can hear the cheering and clapping though.

Dad says, *It's okay,* and I tell him, *I know.*

Over all the noise in the auditorium I can still hear in my head what Devon told me. *I have to go now Scout. I'll be up there. You're going to be just fine.*

I don't know how long I stand there before Michael is pulling on my hand saying, *Caitlin there's cake and lemonade on the lawn!*

What? I ask him. *Why would they put it on the grass?*

He giggles and says, *It's on TABLES on the grass. Come on! Let's get some!*

I look back at Dad who has stopped gripping the armrests and his lips curl up on one side and he says, *Go on Caitlin,* and I run after Michael up the aisle and out the back door of the auditorium and into the sun.

Michael and I are the first ones to the table and we both get edge pieces of cake that have lots of blue and white frosting.

Josh gets one also. Some grown-ups smile at us and tell us we look like middle schoolers with all the blue and white on us. Michael grins and when I see how blue his teeth are I laugh. Even Josh smiles.

Mr. Walters the art teacher comes over while I'm sucking the last glob of blue frosting off of my finger. He hands me a sketchbook and a big box of pastel crayons.

I Look At The Person.

He smiles. *These are for you Caitlin.*

How come?

You gave us all something very special today so I want to give you something.

Thank you, I say, and take the sketchbook. I don't grab the clear plastic box of pastels right away.

I know, he says, *you don't like colors. But I thought you might be ready to give them a try.*

I stare at the colors for a moment. There are three different shades of orange AND lots of reds and yellows so you can make your own orange. And with pastels you can blur them if you want to move from one shade to another. Mr. Walters Gets It. Maybe I can too. Slowly I reach out and take the colors.

Mr. Walters winks. *See you in August.*

Pass it here! Josh shouts, and I turn to see Michael's dad throw Josh a football. After Josh tosses it back Mr. Schneider throws the ball to Dad and he catches it. I forgot that Dad could catch a football. Dad and Devon used to throw a football in the backyard. Sometimes I played too even though I can never catch it until after it hits the ground.

Michael is still next to me but he's stepping from one foot to the other. I can tell that he kind of wants to play football too so I tell him he should follow his empathy and go play. I watch him run and tackle Josh and they both laugh and roll in the grass.

I look down at my shoes and socks. Slowly I push off my shoes and let the cool grass tickle my feet through my socks. Then I bend down and pull my socks off and stand right on top of the grass and the earth and I feel a shiver run up my legs and all the way to my neck and it gives me a little chill. But after I move my feet from side to side a little bit I get used to the prickly cool feeling and it starts feeling softer and more like an okay touch than a tickle.

I walk barefoot over to a big oak tree and sit underneath

it. The breeze blows the leaves around so it's partly shady and partly sunny. I put the sketchbook on my lap and open my new box of colors. Now I'm ready to use them because I figured out how I'm going to draw the whole complete picture. I smile and begin.

Author's Note

The shootings of thirty-three people at Virginia Tech University in Blacksburg, Virginia, on April 16, 2007, were horrible and devastating. While I may not have known those involved personally, it happened in my own backyard. It was the deadliest shooting by a lone gunman in United States history. And wherever or whenever this kind of tragedy occurs, it affects us all. How could something like this happen? Why? What, if anything, could we have done to prevent it? Who knows. But I am certain of one thing. If we all understood each other better, we could go a long way toward stopping violence. We all want to be heard, to be understood. Some of us are better than others at expressing ourselves. Some of us have severe problems that need to be addressed, not ignored, no matter what the cost. Saving society money is a travesty if the cost of that savings is in human lives. *Ignore* and *ignorance* share the same root.

This book was inspired by the events at Virginia Tech as well as my own need to try to explain what it's like for a child to have Asperger's syndrome. The two themes are related in my mind because I believe strongly in early intervention, whatever the disability. Understanding people's difficulties and—just as crucial—helping people understand their own difficulties *and* teaching them concrete ways to help themselves will help them better deal with their own lives and, in turn, ours. In this novel, the main character has Asperger's syndrome but is receiving early intervention through the public school system. She has only one parent and he is far from perfect. Her brother was the family member who really listened to her, tried to understand her, and taught her helpful behavioral skills. Unfortunately, he is killed in a school shooting, and now, but for her school counselor, she is on her own. I hope that, by getting inside her head, readers will understand seemingly bizarre behavior. And I hope that readers will see that, by getting inside someone's head, really understanding that person, so many misunderstandings and problems can be avoided—misunderstandings and problems that can lead to mounting frustration and, sometimes, even violence.